ARISE

LEGACY OF FLAMES
BOOK TWO

EMMA L. ADAMS

1

———

"**I**f you can't take the heat, stay away from the enraged dragon."

It was with those words that I addressed the giant tentacled monster that had wrapped itself around a middle-aged woman carrying a shopping bag and was slowly squeezing the life out of her.

"Help!" screamed the woman, clinging onto a lamp post with both hands as she attempted to climb to safety. "The shadows are eating me!"

A few years ago, uttering that phrase in the middle of London would have resulted in raised eyebrows and the assumption that one was drunk or confused, but the majority of London's human population had seen their worldview upended since an army of invaders from the fae realm had steamrollered through the city and brought all manner of impossible creatures out of hiding. Two years on, supernaturals like me were now able to live out in the open without concealing ourselves from our human neighbours, but man-eating monsters were as common a sight as pigeons in

Trafalgar Square and with significantly more claws and teeth. This one had neither but instead resembled a shadowy mass of tentacles with a habit of spitting ambulant slime to paralyse its victims. Lovely.

I reached for my knife. Iron or steel was always a sure bet when faced with any kind of fae beast, but I'd have to be careful to avoid hurting the victim while I took it down. On the woman's other side, Becks stood in wait, ready to transform into a cat, if need be. Will had taken the job of watching over Cori, my sister, who'd been unconscious since we'd rescued her from the Orion League's prison two weeks ago. As a result of trading shifts on watch duty, we had to fight monsters as a two-person team rather than three.

Knife in hand, I swiped at a tentacle. Despite its semi-transparency, the iron sliced straight through, and the severed tentacle dropped into the road. Becks cut in with a knife in each hand—kitchen knives, but they'd do the job—and severed another tentacle, but the monster had at least twenty and the woman was running out of oxygen fast.

Taking careful aim, I stabbed at the tentacle wrapped around her back. Shadow shrivelled to grey ash as the iron took effect. The woman wriggled free, and I seized the chance to aim at the pulsing mass visible beneath the tentacles.

The creature spat at me, a wad of viscous black slime that hit the pavement and reared up like a fast-growing plant in an attempt to grab my ankles. As I backtracked, Becks reached the monster's exposed core. Her twin knives struck home, and the creature collapsed into a mass that shrank inward until nothing was left but a greyish stain on the pavement.

The woman screamed again. Her arms were lifted above her head, and from the angle of her body, something invisible had grabbed her.

Ah, shit. Even shifters didn't have the Sight—the ability to see through faerie glamour—and neither Becks nor I had seen the monster had brought backup.

I left the tentacled creature lying in a heap and aimed at the new target, but my knife passed through empty air. Becks shouted a warning as a burst of light revealed a spindly fae creature, its hook-like hands releasing the woman and reaching for my throat.

I raised my own hands in defence—hands now turned into red-scaled claws—and caught the creature's hand before it reached my neck. My claws ripped through its stick-like form, and it collapsed into two halves upon the pavement.

The woman pointed at my claws, her mouth hanging open like a drawbridge. Ah, dammit. I'd been doing my level best to fly under the radar—pun intended—since I'd been all over the local news a few weeks ago. A dragon on the front page tends to stick in the mind.

I sheepishly hid my hands behind my back and put on an unconvincing smile. "Just a new spell my witch friend is working on."

In fairness, Will probably *could* manufacture a spell that conjured up scaled gloves if the mood took him, but he'd spent the best part of the past fortnight rebuilding his supplies after his shop had been trashed by the very people responsible for forcing me to expose my dragon side to the world. Funny how the papers had never mentioned that part.

Instead, I'd since been replaced with the usual stories, like gargoyle gangs brawling in Soho, a kraken in the Thames, and a chimera in Green Park. But not a peep about the Orion League. No mention of the sinister underground prison in which they'd experimented on shifters and turned us against one another. Not a word of how they'd kidnapped my sister, and my friends and I had rescued her from certain death. The only allusion to the League's leader, Malkin, had been an anonymous account of how my friends and I had trashed his fancy house in our bid to rescue Cori.

The fact that Cori had been in a coma ever since her rescue had thrown a bucket of icy water over our victory, and my constant state of nervousness about her plight did nothing to help my intention to keep my dragon side under wraps. I concentrated for several seconds before my claws turned back into regular human hands and I was able to help Becks pull out the bin bags she'd brought to transport the dead monster back to the local clean-up unit.

That was what we did for a living these days: killed monsters for a pittance. And for the added security of knowing one fewer human-eating menace was loose on the street, I supposed. It beat starving on the streets, but I'd be willing to endure worse if only my sister were at my side. Leaving her at home dug into my conscience like a rusty nail in my shoe, but staying at her comatose side brought out my temper in a worse way, and the others had grown tired enough of my agitated hovering to drag me out of the house whenever possible.

"Delightful creatures." Becks stashed her knives away and lifted a bin bag to dispose of the hook-handed fae first. She was an unassuming sight in her human form, maybe five feet tall with deep tanned skin and hair striped in an ombre black-brown effect that matched the markings on her cat form. "Now let's get that tentacled thing out of here."

Easier said than done. Shoving a mass of tentacles and dead skin into a bin bag while avoiding the slime it had left on the pavement was like wrestling a giant slug, and the revolting ooze soon covered both of us from head to toe. When we'd finally sealed the bag on our revolting haul, the woman handed a ten-pound note to Becks. "For your trouble."

She avoided my eyes, probably still unsettled by my claws. I tried not to feel too insulted. At least she hadn't tried to hit me over the head with a fire extinguisher like one of our previous clients had. And she'd given us a tip, too.

Becks and I split the bags between us and began the long and torturous task of hauling our cargo down the street. Being Londoners who'd spent most of our lives in hiding, none of my friends could drive, and taking dead faeries on public transport or in taxis was frowned upon, for obvious reasons. The local pickup was a good half-hour away made longer depending on how many bags of dead monster we had to haul. What the mercenaries' clean-up crew did with the bodies, I absolutely did not want to know.

"What do you want to spend the extra tenner on?" asked Becks. "We can split it four ways or buy something all of us will use."

"What, like weapons? Or decent food for once?" *It's not like Cori's awake to enjoy it,* said a cynical voice in my head which had been getting increasingly hard to ignore in recent days. "If you ask me, the guild ought to pay us twice over for bagging two monsters and not one."

"Buy one monster, get one free," Becks quipped. "I bet they'll pull out some bullshit rule on us again that cheats us out of half the money."

"That's what we get for going official." We'd scraped together a living for the last two years through taking on odd jobs, since our former lives had gone up in smoke along with half the city. After our last independent mission had led the hunters right to our doorstep, we'd signed up with the local mercenary unit to lessen the odds of someone trying to knife us in the back. Except the monsters we hunted, that is.

Most people would pick a less hazardous way to make a living, but shifters had possibly even less chance of being hired than other supernaturals did, for the depressing reason that some of us were easily mistaken for the shape-changing beasts who'd invaded the Earth. The only way to prove ourselves trustworthy was to fight *against* the faeries who'd caused so much damage to the world. And try not to get eaten in the process.

My arms were numb by the time we reached the pickup spot, an old warehouse covered in laminated posters advertising employment at the local guild of mercenaries. The term 'guild' was self-appointed and half the time wasn't even spelled right on the posters, for all their proclamations of being proudly in line with the Mage Lords' long-term plan to clean up London's streets so people could leave their houses without being eaten alive.

Becks rolled her eyes at the posters. "I notice nobody's put a bounty on the League members yet, even though they're the ones who set a giant robot on the loose in the city."

"Malkin never showed himself in person, though," I reminded her. "A lot of the others wore masks. I guess it's kinda hard to put out arrest warrants on people who all look identical."

That, and I'd roasted half of them alive when they'd cornered me in Magic Avenue. There was a good reason I'd been avoiding the place for two weeks. Turning into a dragon in front of one's neighbours makes for some awkward conversations.

"Where in the world is the pickup crew?" Becks said, depositing the bin bag in the designated area by the warehouse with a revolted look on her face. There were already a sizeable number of equally disgusting bags and sacks in the vicinity. "It looks like nobody's been here in a week."

"No clue." I didn't particularly want to go *into* the warehouse, because it smelled like a troll had curled up and died in it and then been left to rot for a week. Eyes watering from the stench, I backed away from the revolting pile of monster parts and turned to Becks. "I'm going to report this to old Harwood. He'll bitch at me, but honestly. I know watching a bunch of decomposing faeries isn't a nice job, but if they stay there much longer, they'll attract a horde of redcaps and worse."

"True." Becks gave the warehouse one last look of disgust and turned away.

It took a further fifteen minutes to reach the office of the local mercenary unit, but at least we weren't carrying a sack of tentacles this time around. Such places had sprung up all over the city when it had become clear that the monsters who'd accompanied the invading Sidhe were here to stay and not at all picky about their taste in cuisine.

The office had once been a bank, but someone had stripped down the signs and replaced them with a crooked handmade plaque declaring this to be the "Mersenerry Gild." I hadn't wanted to get on the wrong foot with our new employer by pointing out the errors, but old Harwood wasn't exactly known for attention to detail.

We found the boss at his usual place behind a crooked desk. He was a middle-aged guy with pasty skin that looked like he'd never seen the sun and thinning brown hair laced with grey. For some reason, the mercenary units attracted people who'd survived the invasion by sheer luck and didn't want to risk their necks, so they'd taken on admin positions to make other people risk their necks instead. They were almost always unpleasant. Old Harwood wasn't the worst boss I'd had, but his current expression was more akin to a manager about to fire us than someone greeting two employees who'd completed a successful project.

"Hey." I gave him a smile, which he didn't return. "We just

dropped off the dead faeries at the warehouse. There were two of them, did you know?"

"No," he said. A lie, no doubt. "What was your name again?"

"Caroline," I said, using my current alias. My auburn hair was now jet black, thanks to hair dye, which made me a little less recognisable than before, and it was lucky the cameras which had snapped dozens of photos of me in dragon form hadn't recorded what I looked like as a human.

"Surname?"

"Hicks. Why?"

"New policy." His gaze shifted to Becks. "Alice, is it?"

"Yes." Her eyes narrowed. "What policy?"

"We need to see official ID from all employees," he said. "Passport, driving licence…"

"I don't drive and I've never left the country." Oh, *shit.*

"Do you have your birth certificate?"

"Who carries their birth certificate around? Besides, I lost it when my house was destroyed two years ago. There's nothing left."

A lie. I'd never had a birth certificate. The notebook I'd arrived in London with listed the eleventh of March as my date of birth and I assumed it was accurate, because I had no memories before I was twelve and Cori was five. The only other information the notebook had given me was a guide on how to survive as a dragon shifter in a world that wanted me dead.

"Then apply for a new one," said Old Harwood. "There's a waiting list. Until then, you're not permitted to take on work from this guild. There are too many people out to take the money and scarper. We're running a business here."

Dammit. What had brought this on? Maybe the mages had given them a shakedown for their lax approach to security, but even they should know that most people had lost everything two years ago and were lucky to have their lives, let alone anything else.

"Never mind," I said. "We'll go somewhere else. Can we have the payment for today?"

"As I said." He crossed his arms. "We're only hiring registered individuals."

I ground my back teeth. "You said there's a waiting list. We already did the work. We need the money today."

I wasn't kidding. We were running low on supplies, and Will hadn't replenished his stock of witch ingredients enough to consider re-opening his shop, which left mercenary work as our only source of income. Yes, the mages had given us a cash reward after Will had pointed them to a lawbreaking witch—the same guy who'd already turned *us* in to the hunters and kickstarted the current shit show that was our lives—but that had only gone so far. There had been a lot of shifters left destitute after we'd rescued them from the Orion Stronghold and the thought of not offering them help after they'd suffered so badly at the hunters' hands had been out of the question.

"Too bad," said old Harwood. "You'll know for next time."

I ground my back teeth. "Who ordered this? The Mage Lords?"

Please say yes. The mages weren't fans of shifters, but they didn't want us dead. Unlike the hunters, who'd have very good reason to have our names and addresses on public record.

"The authorities," said Old Harwood. "Get out. I have work to do."

"Work like moving those dead faeries?" asked Becks. "Why are there so many outside the warehouse? Aren't they supposed to have been removed by now?"

He rose from his seat so that he loomed over us. "Get out."

"But we did the bloody job!" Becks stood her ground, outrage flashing in her eyes.

"And you're unregistered. If you show up here with ID, you'll get your payment."

"That's such bullshit," she exploded. "You should have told us not to take the job if you didn't plan to pay us. We nearly got killed."

"You know what you signed up for."

"Leave it," I muttered to Becks. "It's not worth it." Anything we did to draw attention to ourselves would only come back to bite us.

We'd deliberately picked this outpost of the city's mercenaries because it was as far from our previous haunts as possible. Applying for official ID documents was out of the question. I could think of a few people who would be delighted to find a database listing everyone who was supernatural. I didn't need to make the League's job any easier.

Becks huffed but followed me outside. A few drops of rain fell, and I heaved a sigh at the thought of the long walk home. The bus was an option, but the only cash we had was the tenner the woman had given us, and we were both covered in slime besides. Meanwhile, nobody had cleaned the ghosts out of the Underground yet, so the trains were on pause while necromancers took care of the rampant undead problem.

London had a lot of rebuilding to do. So did the world.

"Bullshit," Becks growled to herself. "Who the hell makes those regulations?"

"It's gotta be the Mage Lords," I said, burying my hands in my pockets. "They can trace their ancestry back for a thousand years or more. They assume all supernaturals are the same and have nothing to hide."

"They've never had to live in the shadows like we have. Though they sure are being elusive. I haven't seen a mage in weeks, and they're meant to be cleaning up this." She waved a hand at the street, on which the mercenary unit was the only building still intact. The road had been cleared of broken glass and debris, but nobody had made any effort to restore the collapsed roofs and shattered windows and a thick layer of neglect smothered everything like low-hanging clouds.

"It really doesn't make sense," I said. "The mercs have got to know half or more of their recruits are supernaturals. Most humans wouldn't sign up to go on monster-catching duty except out of desperation."

"What are they doing, creating a supernatural registry?"

"Bloody hope not." Rain fell, soaking my hair and sliding down the back of my neck. I growled in annoyance. "Wish we could go back underground."

""Me too," Becks said, with feeling.

We'd rarely used our tunnels in the past two weeks. The hunters might not have resurfaced, but the memories of the Stronghold were fresh in all our minds, and the knowledge that they knew all our best hiding places made the risks outweigh the benefits. Most of the time. Dragons didn't like water, and the curtains of rain masking my vision only served to make me more pissed off at the world in general. For all I knew, the hunters were now the ones hiding below the ground.

Yeah, right. They always found it easy to blend in.

Anger churned inside me, tinged with the helplessness I'd become all too accustomed to lately. I'd been counting on today's payment to put towards trying another potion to wake Cori. I'd thought she was suffering from exhaustion or the aftereffects of being drugged when we'd first brought her home, but she hadn't so much as opened an eye since her rescue. The potions we used to keep her alive didn't come cheap, and if not for Will's connections with other witches, we'd have already run out of options.

The galling part was that none of this would have been a problem if not for Malkin's irrational hatred of all supernaturals, especially shifters, and his habit of brainwashing his followers into believing we were pure evil. Some members had had the sense to walk away, like Giselle, who'd been tortured at the League's hands, and Astor, who... well, the less I thought about him the better.

"What now?" Becks said. "We can't go back there. We'll also have to come up with new names, and I've had enough of keeping track of aliases as it is."

"Yeah, I'll have to look at the local job centre."

"I thought we said nothing local."

"We probably won't be sticking around for much longer," I said. "The neighbours are already starting to ask questions. I'm sure they know about our other guest, too."

The guest in question was a half-faerie named Kit who spent half his time shrieking at the wall and the other half muttering to himself in languages none of us knew. He'd been held captive and tortured in the Stronghold for an unknown amount of time and had barely spoken a coherent word to us since we'd got him out.

A shadow flickered in the corner of my eye, and a blurred reflection passed through the nearest window, a short distance behind us.

"Becks," I whispered. "I think we're being followed."

"You're shitting me."

I jerked my head towards the window of the shop we'd just passed. A crack split the glass in two, but the blurred image of a figure clad in black was unmistakeable.

Great. Looks like we're getting into another unpaid fight after all.

My claws itched to come out, but I rested a hand on the knife at my belt instead. The figure disappeared from sight as soon as I tried to get a closer look at his reflection in the glass. He was male—I thought—but surely a hunter would have attacked openly. Playing peekaboo in the pouring rain wasn't their typical style.

"Who's there?" I called out.

No reply. A suspicion latched onto me, and I pushed sodden hair out of my eyes, anger burning brighter than ever. Straightening my shoulders, I began walking again, at speed.

"What're you doing?" Becks asked. "I bet we can corner that guy."

"I can't be arsed, frankly." I surreptitiously peeked at each window we passed, catching the occasional flash of black in the glass but no glimpse of his face. Not that I needed to see any more to identify our pursuer.

Why the hell is he *following us?*

Or rather, why not just talk to me openly? It wasn't like we'd parted on bad terms. At least, I hadn't thought so. It was anyone's guess as to what was going on in *his* head.

"He's still behind us," Becks muttered as we picked up the pace again.

"I know."

"Why not ask what he wants?"

"Clearly he's in assassin mode and doesn't want to talk in public."

He also shouldn't be able to easily keep pace with a pair of shifters, but the highest rank of hunters known as the Elites had been given advantages over regular humans via tattoos that Malkin had gleefully confirmed to be magical in nature. To say Astor hadn't taken that revelation well was an understatement, and I could only assume that was why he'd spent the past fortnight avoiding me.

I unlocked the door, my wet hands fumbling the key as footsteps sounded behind me. Then I turned to see Astor—the man who'd tried to kill me, saved my life more times than

I could count and literally taken a bullet for me—and then, after sharing a bone-melting kiss, had vanished off the face of the earth.

I didn't know what I expected him to say. An apology, maybe. A 'nice to see you'.

What he said instead was "I know how to wake your sister."

2

Astor rested one foot inside the paved front yard and one hand on the gate. His chestnut-brown hair had been cut shorter, presumably by hand, and was stuck to his pale forehead with rainwater. Green eyes assessed me, blinking less frequently than most people I knew. But then, he was hardly a typical human.

And talking utter bollocks. "I'm sorry, what? All the spells and potions we've tried haven't been able to wake her up, and Will's been in touch with the most powerful witches in London."

"That's because the League used a powerful sleeping draught," he said. "One designed to subdue larger creatures."

"Dragons." I took a step back, revulsion rippling through me. "She's a *child*."

"Also, how do you know that?" Becks demanded. "What did you do, help make the drug they used on her?"

"No." Astor's mouth tightened at the edges. "If I'd known that was what they used, I'd have told you sooner. The effect is magnified due to her being in human form and being underage."

"You said you can help." Did I believe him? To say Astor and I had a rocky history would be the understatement of the millennium. Yes, he'd saved my life—and the reverse was true—but a dragon shifter had killed his family, and he'd spent his life training to be a ruthless shifter-killer before changing course and working against the Orion League from the inside. Malkin had nearly had him executed, and after I'd got us both out of the Stronghold alive, I'd thought the two of us had established enough common ground to put our pasts behind us.

Instead, he'd ghosted me for two weeks, and showed up out of nowhere when I was already cranky as fuck and soaked to the skin. My claws pressed against my fingernails, demanding to be sheathed in the next person who pissed me off.

"Get on with it," Becks added. "If they used some kind of powerful tranquiliser on Cori, I take it this isn't the sort that regular humans have access to?"

I bet not. They'd used the witches' own spell ingredients to create magical bullets specially designed to kill supernaturals, and the tattoos they inked on their Elites resembled the glyphs used in some witch spells. Apparently, nobody had ever told Malkin the definition of irony.

"Exactly," said Astor. "I didn't know they were still experimenting with that. None of the test subjects they used it on ever woke up."

Dread pooled at the base of my spine. "Test subjects. Meaning shifters."

"Hunters, too," said Astor.

"If you're playing for sympathy, it won't work," Becks said. "We all know they viewed you all as equally expendable."

"I know they did," he said calmly. "I'm giving some context. After five recruits died of dehydration after being unable to wake up, the League dropped the idea of using a tranquiliser that strong and nobody mentioned it for years. Regardless of what they used on her, I went looking for more information when I found out she hadn't woken up. There were records in the Stronghold saying that something called the Moonbeam can be used as a cure for any ailment affecting a shifter."

Recognition pinged inside the back of my mind. "The Moonbeam?"

Find the moonbeam. The last words the other dragon shifter had said to me seconds before he'd died. I hadn't understood what he meant. I still didn't. Unless he'd known, somehow, that the Moonbeam was what I needed to wake up Cori.

"That's right," said Astor. "Ever since then, I've been trying to find clues as to what it is."

"And where to find it, I assume," Becks said. "Because if this is another one of your elaborate plans that's going to end up with us all nearly getting killed, I think we could all do without the lies and deception this time. Right, Ember?"

I grunted agreement. Despite my best efforts not to let Astor's behaviour get to me, it had been hard not to take his disappearance personally, and even harder not to let the others see how pissed off I was. Between his absence and Cori being in a coma, any patience I might have had for mind games had evaporated.

"Not exactly," he said. "From what I was able to work out, it's a magical artefact that used to be in the possession of the League, but that disappeared in the invasion. Malkin had it in his personal collection."

"And he lost it?" I arched a brow. "Careless of him."

"Stealing magical objects seems to be a running theme with the League," said Becks. "Let me guess, it's still missing?"

"Yes, and when I started asking questions, I ended up

strung from the ceiling by my feet while a bunch of gargoyles threw punches at me."

"You pissed off the gargoyles?" Becks scoffed. "Well done. Why not pick someone less punchy to question?"

"Because the information I found made it pretty clear that the Moonbeam originally belonged to the shifters."

"Of course it bloody well did," I said darkly. "I suppose the League still wants it back."

"Probably," said Astor. "You know they don't let things they believe to be theirs get away easily."

"Like me. And you." Anger coiled in my chest together with the heat that preceded a shift. "They've been awfully quiet lately. Do you know where they are?"

"No," he said. "I was too busy following leads on the Moonbeam. The last rumour I heard pointed to Magic Avenue, but I thought you'd be better equipped to ask questions there than I am."

"That's up to Will, not us." I glanced at Becks. "Nice of you to finally bring us in on your plan. Is that what you've been doing since we left the Stronghold?"

"No, I've been working."

"Honest work?" The thought amused me, for some reason.

"Believe it or not, yes," he said. "I'm a taxi driver."

I stared at him then cracked up laughing. "Pick something more realistic next time."

"I'm telling the truth." A current of irritation underlaid his voice.

"An assassin doing normal people stuff. Doesn't compute." Okay, so he probably had a good enough idea of London's streets, but from scurrying over the rooftops, not getting stuck in traffic. I wouldn't have thought he'd have the patience for it. Though he must have figured out how to scrape together a living somehow, and in the post-invasion world, most people couldn't afford to be picky.

"I'm not an assassin." *Now* he sounded pissed off. Was I being rude? Yes, and he didn't owe me anything, but I wished such a thing as a mind-reading potion existed so that I might have the faintest clue what was going on inside his head.

"Well, we just lost *our* jobs thanks to bureaucratic nonsense, and we don't need you bringing a horde of gargoyles on our tail. Did you learn anything from them while you were hanging upside-down?"

"Actually yes," he replied. "Lost your jobs? What do you mean?"

"Tell us first," Becks broke in. "The gargoyles are masters of gossip. I take it that's why you willingly turned yourself into a punching bag?"

"Right, and I read more between the lines than they said," he said. "The Moonbeam seems to have a powerful effect on shifters. It can boost their strength, as well as curing the effects of virtually any spell or poison. I imagine you won't be the only people hunting for it."

A chill raced between my shoulder blades. "Boosting a shifter's strength? What use would that be to the hunters?"

Or to us, for that matter? A dragon would certainly have no need of it, and all shifters had enhanced speed and strength compared to regular humans. We didn't have the gifts of other supernaturals—necromancers could raise and calm the dead; mages had a single powerful skill like conjuring fire; and witches could use any kind of spell or potion, with a range of specialities—but we didn't need them. We were a force of nature all on our own.

"Malkin certainly wanted it," said Astor. "Whether to keep power out of the shifters' hands or for his own purposes."

"Because he thinks everything belongs to him." My hands fisted. "Well, we'll just have to find it ourselves."

For Cori, and to honour the other dragon shifter's last words. The memory of his death twisted me up inside. Years of imprisonment had left him weakened, confused, barely able to tell friend from foe. We'd nearly killed one another, and knowing there'd been no saving him from the hunters' bullets did nothing to lessen the weight of guilt in my chest. His death had also brought an end to my brief hope that I'd be able to learn where the other dragon shifters were hiding, if any survived. My memories of the years Cori and I had spent with them had been erased by whoever had put us on a train to London eleven years ago. We'd been raised by Rhea, a gargoyle who ran a shelter for displaced shifters and who'd accepted our dragon shifter nature without question, but she'd never been able to tell us how to find the rest of our kind.

"Right." Astor took a step back. "I've told you what I know. I can gather more information, if you like."

"Won't you just do that anyway?"

He had contacts of his own, and probably not on the legal side. I didn't give a crap, in truth, but it unsettled me to think he'd gone back into the Stronghold so soon after its abandonment. Hadn't he been concerned he might run into Malkin or his allies? The hunters did not forgive betrayal, and Astor had committed the worse sin of spending the past two years playing both sides. He'd done so with disturbing conviction, but then, it had been easy to pretend to hate our guts when it had been dragon shifters who'd killed his family.

Maybe I shouldn't have been surprised that he'd wanted to spend as little time around me as possible after the truth had come out.

"What are you standing out in the rain for?" asked a sleepy voice. Will padded barefoot to the door, his blond hair standing on end. He must have been napping to compensate for being on guard duty all night. "Oh. It's you."

"I was leaving," said Astor. "I'll let you know if I find out anything else."

As he turned and left, Will rubbed his eyes. "What did I do?"

"Nothing." I walked after him into the house, trying to suppress my annoyance and being thoroughly unsuccessful. "He's trying to get into our good graces again."

"Not the only place he was trying to get, the last I saw of you two."

"Oi." I trod on his foot.

Will yelped. "Whoa. Twitchy. I was kidding, Ember."

"I'm a little on edge."

"You're also dry," Becks commented. "Why am I soaking wet from the rain and not you?"

"Huh?" My gaze swivelled to the hall mirror. She was right. In the few minutes I'd been standing under the shelter outside the house, my hair had dried and I'd stopped shivering with cold. "Dragon thing, maybe."

One of the perks—or not—of growing up away from my fellow dragon shifters was that I was still learning about the quirks that set me apart from other kinds of shifter. It wasn't like I had a guidebook... well, I did, but it was hardly comprehensive. When I'd first shown up in London, I'd found a notebook in my rucksack, presumably gifted by whoever had put Cori and me on the train. Its contents detailed a few ways in which dragons were different than regular shifters, but half the pages were empty, and the rest contained a few lines of text in a language I didn't know and had never been able to translate.

Will entered the small downstairs flat we'd chosen as a temporary base until we deemed it safe to return to Magic Avenue. Rent was dirt cheap on account of the upstairs floor being in ruins and the roof caved in, but it otherwise seemed sturdy enough, and we'd put iron wards on the ceiling to stop any man-eating fae from surprising us during the night. By mutual assent, we'd put Cori and Kit's mattresses in the living room while the three of us were crammed into the sole bedroom so that the half-faerie's habit of yelling in his sleep didn't keep us awake.

My sister, by contrast, hadn't uttered a sound since her rescue. Cori lay still, curled on the mattress I'd brought out for her with a cloud of auburn hair covering her face. My heart tied itself in a knot. I hated that I couldn't do anything to help her.

Or maybe I could.

"Have you heard of the Moonbeam?" I asked Will. "Astor claims it can wake up Cori."

"Nope. What is it, an antidote?"

"No, an artefact," I replied. "Allegedly. Malkin had it, but it went missing during the invasion."

"And Astor really thinks it will cure her?"

"I don't think we should listen to him," Becks said. "Anything that guy says is suspect."

"He has no reason to hide the truth now." I swivelled to Will. "The trouble is, he claims that the last rumour he heard about the Moonbeam pointed to Magic Avenue."

"Oh."

"Exactly."

The Avenue was still a sore point with him. While Will's shop had suffered remarkably little damage from the hunters' attack, the fact that one of his own neighbours had turned us over to the hunters had been an unsettling reminder that even the witches didn't all see shifters as their equals. And though Twill had been hauled off by the mages on unrelated charges, the memory of me shifting into a dragon publicly would be too fresh in the minds of residents to risk going back.

"I mean, it's safer than going into a gargoyles' nest like Astor did."

"Is that what he's been doing since we blew up the Stronghold?" Will said. "Let me guess, they threw him out the window?"

"Hung him upside-down from the ceiling, but close enough," I replied. "I don't know why he didn't tell us earlier, since the Moonbeam's supposedly valuable to shifters. And—the other dragon told me to *Find the Moonbeam*. Those were his last words."

"Oh." Becks chewed her lower lip. "Yeah, that's reason enough to take a closer look. Though if everyone else is supposedly after this Moonbeam, we'll have to tread carefully."

"What do the gargoyles want with it?" asked Will. "Magical objects that can awaken someone from a coma seems like a niche market. Unless there are bunch of people stuck in an enchanted sleep without a prince to kiss them awake."

I snorted. "According to Astor, the Moonbeam also gives shifters a power boost. Not sure how it works."

"And you believe him."

"He has no reason to lie." Nor to offer us help, but maybe he felt he owed me a debt, after I'd got him out of the Stronghold alive. "If we're going to check out this rumour, we need to decide who goes and who'll stay behind."

"I have more of a reason for visiting the Avenue than you two," Will said. "Plus, you know, one of us is significantly more conspicuous than the others."

"Yeah." I ran my teeth over my lower lip. "The thing is, the other dragon shifter… he used his last words to ask me to find the Moonbeam. I might not know what he meant, but it feels like the Moonbeam might have some special significance for us. For the dragon shifters, that is."

There was an awkward silence. The others might have a shifter's understanding of what it was to be an outsider, but not the loneliness that came from being among the last of my kind. For all I knew, the other dragon shifters hadn't even survived the invasion, though I wanted to believe they had. Malkin had claimed that dragons could even face up to the Sidhe—the all-powerful faeries who'd invaded this realm and left it in ruins—but I'd never seen the proof. He'd also claimed that the dragon shifters were warmongers who'd driven each other to extinction more effectively than the hunters ever could.

A lie, like everything he said. Dragon shifters had their flaws, sure. We could be overprotective, stubborn, reckless, violent even... but in the end, the League were the real monsters. All we wanted was to live.

I looked down at Cori's face, smoothed in the illusion of a peaceful slumber. Malkin had told me explicitly that he didn't need more than one dragon shifter and that even if I'd willingly cooperated with him, he'd have kept her there in a state of unconsciousness indefinitely. He'd never wanted her to wake up.

Screw that. I'd find the Moonbeam, even if I had to strip it from Malkin's corpse, and then Cori and I would finish off the League for good.

3

After a brief debate over whether to approach Magic Avenue via the hidden tunnel that came out into Will's basement, we opted to take the scenic route instead. Meaning Will flew to Trafalgar Square while I clung to his back and hoped that nobody would look close enough to spot me hiding behind his feathered wings. Gargoyles weren't exactly known for being placid and easy-going steeds.

The National Gallery was remarkably intact compared to its surroundings, though I suspected the mages had had a hand in protecting the exhibits from the destruction wrought during the faerie invasion. The surrounding streets had been cleaned of broken glass and abandoned vehicles, but the lion statues by the fountain had gone. There was some speculation about whether they'd been gargoyles in disguise. Anything was possible. The pubs, meanwhile, were packed with people sheltering from the rain. Some things never changed.

Magic Avenue was sandwiched between two streets near Charing Cross, protected by iron wards to keep out the fae.

It had also once been concealed by a spell that hid it from human eyes but was no longer necessary in the post-invasion world. Any human who unthinkingly wandered inside often fled as soon as they saw the first explosion—and as the Avenue was inhabited mostly by witches who home-brewed their spells, that tended to happen a lot.

Witch spells were in high demand even among humans, but most shops on the Avenue catered to supernaturals alone, selling base ingredients that weren't much use outside of the hands of a practitioner. Like most witches, Will could do a lot with the bare minimum and could probably cobble together a spell out of spiderwebs and a piece of chewing gum if he put his mind to it, but high-end spells like illusions were out of reach without the more expensive ingredients. I'd assumed the same would be true of whatever cure we needed to save Cori, but that it instead required a unique object seemingly sought after by hunters and shifters alike was yet another addition to the pile of shit the universe had seen fit to dump on our heads in the past few weeks.

I didn't hold out too much hope we'd find any clues in the Avenue—the few other shifter residents would have run for the hills as soon as the hunters started burning their houses down—but we had to start somewhere.

"I think someone's throwing a party," Will remarked when we glimpsed the flicker of bright lights around the corner of the Avenue. "That or a witch has decided to try and make the elixir of life again."

"Hopefully the former." As the first group of supernaturals to suffer open persecution among humans, many witches didn't advertise their supernatural nature even with magic an everyday sight to most people. But on this street, they did so with pride, at least when the hunters weren't stomping around breaking everything. A lights display wasn't unusual, but as we followed the winding street, the smell of smoke tickled my nostrils. *Oh, no. There's trouble.*

Twill's shop was on fire. The whole building had ignited, flames licking at the windows and threatening to spill over to its neighbouring rooftops. A couple of locals had brought out a large hosepipe, but the foaming spray of water wasn't enough to dampen the blaze.

"Oh, shit." I slowed my pace. "So much for us raiding his cupboards."

"D'you think Twill was in there?" Will asked hopefully.

"Not if the mages locked him in prison," I reminded him. "I thought his place already burned down."

"Guess the hunters were feeling generous that day."

Some of the other shops hadn't been so lucky. Charred doors hung from their hinges on several buildings, and there was a general lack of customers wandering the street. I'd been so wrapped up in looking after Cori and keeping a roof over our heads in the last few weeks that I'd had little time to consider the mess we'd left behind us after I'd obliterated the automaton and sent the hunters fleeing from the street.

"Who did it?" I murmured, treading closer. "Do you think it was a disgruntled neighbour mad at him for calling the hunters, or...?"

"Or they're back?" Will blanched. "They can't be... Ember, what are you doing?"

I peered into the alley that ran alongside the house, noting that a downstairs window lay open. "I wonder if Twill left evidence behind?"

"Please don't run into a burning building."

"I'm pretty sure I can't catch on fire." Granted, we hadn't used shadow spells to hide ourselves like we usually did, but my dyed hair made me less recognisable to anyone who might be watching from the windows. "Because, you know. Dragon."

"What if your clothes burn off?" Will protested. "Besides, the person who set the fire might still be around."

"True," I relented. "We can at least check out your shop while we're here."

"Already did. It's fucked." Will's uncharacteristic scowl spoke to his fury at the hunters for vandalising his home. Not just because it was our main base, but because his witch mother had left the premises to him after her death. Since his gargoyle father had died when he was a kid and his mother had raised him alone, the shop had been all he'd had left of his family. But this wasn't the first time the hunters had trashed the place. In fact, the very reason Becks, Cori and I had ended up as Will's housemates was due to us accidentally trespassing in his basement during an ongoing feud between the local gargoyles and the Orion League and witnessing their first unsuccessful attempt to trample all over the residents of Magic Avenue. Like the last time, I was more than happy to help Will rebuild his shop and business and see to it that the League never barged in again.

"We already walked here," I pointed out. "We can check on any supplies you left behind."

"I took everything worth carrying," Will said, angling himself instead towards the two witches holding the hosepipe. "Let's see if anyone knows who torched Twill's place. I think it was a neighbour, personally. Maybe I'll go and thank them."

As he began to walk, I hung back. Out of the corner of my eye, I glimpsed a black-clad figure slink into an alleyway between houses. Astor. *What's he doing here?*

I caught up to Will and tapped him on the shoulder, nodding towards the alley. "Our friend is back."

"*Your* friend," he said. "What's he doing, chatting to locals?"

"I'd ask, but I'm supposed to be keeping a low profile."

The witches with the hosepipe had seen Will and while I kept my head down as I approached him, everyone on the street would know the three shifters he hung out with.

Will sighed. "Call it intuition, but I brought one shadow spell. You can have it if you promise to be good."

"When have I ever got you into trouble?"

"You really want me to answer that? Be careful." He handed me the band-shaped spell.

I slid it onto my wrist and hit the built-in switch that caused the spell's effect to spread over my body, effectively turning me into a shadowy cut-out that was virtually invisible in darkness and hard to see in daytime unless I stood under direct sunlight. With London's sky almost always draped in clouds, keeping hidden wasn't an issue, and I was more confident walking out in the open.

The cobbles were slick with rainwater, forcing me to slow my pace to avoid slipping, but Astor didn't seem to have that problem. As I watched, he skirted the burning building, eyeing the flames as if he wanted to climb inside but couldn't work out how to do so without getting himself burned to a crisp.

Behind me, I heard Will's voice speaking to Keira, one of the witches who'd brought out the hosepipe. She was a middle-aged black woman with greying hair who sold spell ingredients at discounted rates to people she liked, which included Cori and me. In other words, she was very unlikely to be the person who'd started the fire.

"You didn't see anyone in the house?" Will was asking her. "Or hanging around outside?"

"No, I didn't," she said. "I've been sheltering from this ghastly weather."

The fire didn't seem to be hampered by the rain, and only the witches' efforts with the hosepipe had stopped it from spreading to its neighbour. Keira's companion, a plump

Asian woman with glittering decorative spells woven into her hair, shook her head at the flames. "I'd just cleaned up the damage the smoke did to my house after the last time a house caught fire down here. Bloody pranksters."

"You think someone was pulling a prank?" Will asked. "Not arson? I mean, the hunters rampaged down half the street a few weeks ago."

"Including your place," said Keira. "Is that why I haven't seen your friends lately?"

Oh no. I stood as still as possible, aware that the effects of the shadow spell wouldn't last longer than an hour, and witches had sharp eyes for this kind of illusion. Since Keira lived on the opposite street, she might not have seen my shifter form, especially if she'd been hiding indoors, but I was kind of surprised she hadn't heard a rumour at the very least.

"Yeah." Will's voice sounded strained. "I'm still rebuilding my stock, but you know, this isn't exactly encouraging me to move back. Twill's going to be pissed off when he gets out of the mages' lockup and finds his place torched."

"Don't you know he's dead?" said Keira's companion.

Will's breath caught. "What?"

He's dead? I stared at her, resisting the urge to switch off the shadow spell and ask a few questions of my own.

"Yes, they found his body in the river the other morning," Keira said.

"Damn." Will sucked in a breath. "I thought he was in jail."

"The mages changed his sentence to a fine," she said. "I think he'd have been safer in captivity, to tell you the truth."

"What do you mean?" Will asked. "Was it the League who killed him? To tidy up loose ends?"

"Loose ends?" she echoed. "No, I imagine it was whoever he owed that debt to. Fool was playing with fire. Enough that someone decided to make that literal."

I couldn't restrain my curiosity, and evidently, neither

could Astor. He'd moved into the mouth of the alley, seemingly oblivious to the burning house inches away from him, his head tilted towards the witches.

"Shit," said Will quietly. "I knew he sold us out to the League, but…"

"I imagine he did that to pay his debts, too," Keir said gravely. "If I were you, I'd stay out of this one. It's bad news all around."

Will fell silent. His expression showed a mixture of anger and confusion, and I fervently wished Astor wasn't here to overhear this, too. It was hardly his business, but he'd got entangled in the whole mess when he'd tailed the hunters on their mission to capture a dragon shifter. A mission only possible because Twill had given our information to the hunters in exchange for… well, not getting his house set on fire, I supposed.

I hadn't had much direct experience of the supernatural underworld of London, but I'd have to be living under a rock not to have known it had existed since long before the invasion. Rhea had helped many a shifter escape its clutches. Twill had probably owed money to someone dangerous, but it still left a bad taste in my mouth to know that he'd thought it was worth selling out his fellow supernaturals to save himself.

"Any chance you know *who* he owed this debt to?" Will asked.

"No, and I don't care to ask," Keira said. "I wouldn't either, if I were you."

I'd heard enough. Astor clearly didn't care to come out and ask questions, but if he wanted to get into Twill's shop, he must have a reason. Perhaps I'd find something useful in there, too, like evidence pointing to whoever Twill owed a debt to. Any possible link to the Moonbeam was tangential at best, but hadn't that been precisely why Astor had advised us to come back to the Avenue? The underground market did run a trade in rare magical artefacts as well as their other activities.

Maybe the Moonbeam had passed through their hands, too.

As I drew nearer to the house, the burning smell dove into my lungs, threatening to make me cough. It was uncomfortably reminiscent of how I'd nearly choked to death on poison gas back in the Orion Stronghold, and while I was more resilient than a human, I wasn't sure how that extended to non-dragon-related fires.

I peered into the alley and saw Astor was no longer there. Hoping he hadn't gone inside the house himself, I found an open window and pulled myself in. The fire must have started on the upper level, because the shop itself remained untouched despite the thickening smoke in the air. All the shelves were empty—evidently, looters had already been at the place—but if Twill was anything like most witches I knew, he'd have gone to a great deal of trouble to protect his records. Especially if there was something incriminating in there.

Reaching the front counter, I climbed over and began opening drawers. No heat seared my hands, but my eyes watered from the smoke, making it hard to read the files inside. Coughing, I stashed everything I could grab inside my jacket and then ran for the open window before my oxygen ran out.

Once outside, my lungs expanded, taking in air. I shoved a fist in my mouth to mask my coughing fit and looked for Astor. Still no sign of him. Maybe he hadn't gone into Twill's house after all.

The sound of beating wings made me lift my head. A large winged shadow passed above the street, visible in the gap between houses. *A gargoyle?* Not Will, I didn't think, but I ducked out of the alley and saw no signs of him on the ground.

My shadow spell wouldn't last much longer, so I headed towards Will's house to wait it out. The windows were boarded but not broken and the displays removed to discourage looters from breaking in. The tunnel entrance in the basement had been intact the last I'd checked, but the mere thought of walking into the dark conjured up images of the elevator descending through the earth, into the heart of the Orion Stronghold.

"Ember." Will entered the shop. "Thought I saw your shadow roaming around."

"Where've you been?" I asked hoarsely. "I thought you and Astor had run away together."

"I'd rather put a screwdriver through my eyeballs. Also, please tell me you didn't go inside Twill's place."

"I swiped his records." I patted my jacket. "Where *is* Astor?"

"Buggered off back to whatever hole in the ground he's living in now."

"Speaking of holes in the ground, I want to go back through the tunnels." I didn't, but I refused to let the hunters scare me into avoiding our old haunts any longer. "I'm pretty sure I saw a gargoyle on the roof, and if it wasn't you…"

"Dammit," he said. "Don't tell me the gangs are back."

"I only saw one, but I wonder if they're who Twill owed money to."

Most of the rumours I'd heard concerning the magical revolved around the gargoyles. Some of that might be because they were notorious gossips and had the advantage of being able to perch on rooftops and listen in on conversations without anyone being any the wiser. But all rumours started somewhere.

"Hope not." Will pulled a face. "Doesn't excuse him ratting

us out to the hunters, either. Tell you what, I'll take to the sky and see if I can find who it was."

"You sure?" I wouldn't be able to go with him. Taking a human for a piggyback, even another shifter, was generally a no-no in gargoyle culture. "All right. I'll meet you on the other side."

"Be careful in there," he warned. "I haven't been down there since we left, and anyone else might have moved in."

"You be careful, too." The gargoyles could be territorial bastards, and as one himself, Will would be the first to agree. "See you soon."

In the meantime, I needed to get home and see if Twill's papers offered any answers.

4

The journey through the tunnels was surprisingly
uneventful. Our most recent clash with the hunters
had mostly taken place on the surface, and the few
League members who'd followed us underground had met a
grisly fate in a troll's nest. Although our current house was a
long walk from the Avenue, it was nice to have an hour or so
to myself. It felt like I was always either watching my sister
or running errands. Or hunting monsters for the mercenary
guild. *Guess that isn't happening any longer,* I thought,
pondering on where and how to find a new employer. One
who didn't ask the wrong questions. It came down to
whether old Harwood's orders were a city-wide directive or
some unwelcome whim. For all our sakes, I hoped it was the
latter.

Will still wasn't back when I reached the house. He didn't
return until nearly two hours later, when Becks and I were
going through Twill's documents on the living room sofa.
Both of us jumped to our feet when Will stormed in, dripping rainwater everywhere. "Bloody gargoyles."

I gave him a quick check for injuries and then sat back down. "What's with the dramatics?"

He sneezed. "I tailed the guy from Magic Avenue for a bit, but I lost him somewhere along the waterfront. It's hard to follow by air when there are so many other gargoyles swooping around."

"Any idea who it was?" asked Becks, who I'd filled in on our misadventures on Magic Avenue as soon as I'd got back.

"Not anyone I recognise." Will spotted the papers strewn on the floor in front of the sofa. "What's all that?"

"Twill's records," I said. "All his transactions for the last few years. Thought they might tell us what he was mixed up in that made him think selling us out to the hunters was the only way to survive."

Will crouched down to peer at the scattered pages. "There's a fair chance it was the gargoyles, but they don't usually have much use for potions."

"He *was* selling to the hunters." The trouble was, as I'd swiftly found out, the League used aliases when making everyday purchases, and neither Becks nor I had been able to work out which listings might refer to them. "I haven't found any references to the Moonbeam yet, but we found a few items of interest."

"Like?"

"Someone *really* needed a weekly supply of magical lubricant."

Will rolled his eyes. "Sorry, Ember, but I think you're looking in the wrong place. If you want clues about this Moonbeam, I doubt you'll find any in Twill's papers. The old sod mostly traded in potions."

"Did you ask anyone on the Avenue if they'd heard the same rumour Astor did?" I asked. "I mean, he claimed the Moonbeam was last seen on Magic Avenue, and as soon as we got there, the place went up in flames. Both are linked to the Orion League. Hard to put that down to coincidence."

"Keira didn't hear anything, but she also didn't notice Ember shift into a dragon two weeks ago, so I don't think she's been paying much attention."

"Sensible of her. I doubt we're going to find anything useful in here." Becks waved a wad of paper in the air. "We already knew Twill was in trouble with someone dangerous. Someone he was more scared of than he was of the hunters. That's reason enough for us to back off before we find our own shop put to the torch."

"What else is there to do?" I shifted a stack of papers aside and heaved a sigh. "We have no other leads."

"Didn't Astor also say the Moonbeam went missing in the invasion?" Will queried. "That implies someone on the inside nicked it from Malkin. Maybe Astor himself."

"Or Giselle." In fact, hadn't she been his captive during the invasion? Stealing his valuable magical artefacts on the way out sounded like exactly the sort of thing she'd do. "Dammit. Wish Astor had stuck around. I haven't a clue where he's hiding out now."

I'd have to wait until he deigned to show up in person again. Irritated, I shuffled the papers and nearly dropped them when the word *moonbeam* skimmed across my vision. I flicked back through the pages until I found the right one. "Moonbeam leaves. Twill sold someone moonbeam leaves."

"Shifter bait." Becks sprang off the sofa with a curse. "Fuck me, it was Twill who sold the bait to the hunters as well as telling tales on us?"

"I'd bet my scales he did." I swept the papers aside with my fist. "Drowning in the river is too nice a death for him, if you ask me."

"He didn't drown," Will said. "I asked a few questions on the way back, and it sounds like someone slit his throat and threw him in the Thames. He was only found because he washed up on the embankment when a couple of the mages were passing by and spoiled the nice view."

"Who'd you ask?" Becks asked curiously. "Not the gargoyles?"

"Who else has the best lookout posts?" he said. "Don't worry, none of my acquaintances are involved in whatever shady shit got Twill thrown in the river. They're the ones who saw the mages pull out the body. None has any idea who did it. Might have been the hunters, might have been whoever he owed money to. Either way, there's no trail."

"And Astor didn't mention it." Had he known? More to the point, why hadn't he acknowledged me when he'd known full well that Will and I were at the Avenue and were aware of him watching us? Was this how things were going to be now? We'd gone through hell together and yet he was acting like we were acquaintances at best, or that we'd had nothing but a brief fling. An old flame. Ha. If his friend Giselle had indeed been the one to steal the Moonbeam, though, I might have to swallow my pride and seek him out. Wherever he was hiding.

There came an almighty crash. We all leapt to our feet as the window shattered, spraying glass all over the living room, and two men climbed in. Both were heavily muscled and craggy-featured, which would have been clue enough as to their supernatural type without seeing their third hulking companion outside the house resembling nothing so much as a massive winged statue. *Gargoyles.*

"Hands up, all of you," barked the first guy, a giant of a man with shoulders wider than the door and his long blond hair tied back in a ponytail.

"Ah," said Will.

"Will," I hissed. "What in the world did you do?"

"I think they saw me flying around their territory."

"You're joking."

His companion, a pale man with dark sideburns, advanced on us with a knife in his hand. "You trespassed on our territory. Now you're going to come with us."

"Er, no," I said. "We haven't the slightest idea what you're talking about."

"Who're you?" said the dark-haired man. "You look familiar. Are you famous?"

"Definitely not. I'm nobody." Not my best line, but between dragging a bag full of slimy tentacles across the city and trekking back from Magic Avenue via the tunnels, I was too exhausted for a standoff.

"Everyone knows this one"—the blond man jabbed Will in the chest with his index finger—"hangs around with shifter-killing scum."

"You're dead wrong." Will tried to lean out of the way. "Shifter killers? We *are* shifters."

"We saw you flying on our territory," he said. "Just before we found the dead body of one of our own."

We all stared at him. Was he serious? Given the knife and the threatening posture… yes, apparently.

"What?" said Will. "I didn't kill anyone."

"Everyone knows your friend sold shifters out to the League," the blond dude said, grabbing Will by the scruff of the neck and giving him a shake. "Your friend owed us money, and instead, he stabbed us in the back."

"Twill is absolutely not our friend." He was a witch merchant, though, and the gargoyles had seemingly lumped him and Will into the same category on principle. No wonder Twill had been scared enough to rat us out to the hunters if these were the people he was doing business with. "I take it you're the ones who dumped him in the Thames?"

In answer, the blond guy turned into a gargoyle right there in the middle of the living room. Clawed feet tore through carpet, and his six-six frame grew another half-foot, his horned head stooped under the low ceiling. The lightbulb swung alarmingly, while his hunched wings extended, sending the papers I'd taken from Twill fluttering in all directions. It was a good job there wasn't anyone else in the flat upstairs, because if he reared up to his full height, his head would have gone straight through the ceiling.

I took a step back, acutely conscious of Cori lying unconscious in the corner. "Look, we don't want a fight—"

The gargoyle hit me. The blow sent me flying back all the way across the room. I hit the door frame with a thud that knocked the wind from me. Gasping for air, I caught my balance as Will turned into his gargoyle form and flew at the oncoming gargoyle. He only got one punch in before he, too, was thrown bodily into the wall. I winced. Will was small for a gargoyle, being half-witch, and he didn't have a chance against these brutes. Becks's cat form was good at biting and scratching, neither of which was much help against creatures made of stone. As for me? Shifting in here would blow what was left of the roof off.

The other gargoyle transformed, too, his blocky outline obstructing the shattered window. The knife slid from his now-larger hand, but his claws were more than lethal enough on their own. *Oh, bugger.*

A loud wail cut through the air. The ruckus had woken Kit, and the gargoyles stared around in search of the noise. The faerie, whose mattress lay behind the sofa, had sat upright, shrieking in terror. One of the gargoyles let out a growl that I could easily translate as *What the hell is that racket?*

"We have a faerie," I warned them. "And you just woke him up."

Becks turned into a cat and hopped onto the sofa with a

threatening hiss. The faerie let out another high-pitched wail —and then vanished.

Everyone stared at the spot where he'd disappeared. I leapt over to Cori's mattress a heartbeat before the gargoyles launched themselves across the room again. One swiped at Becks, missing by inches, while the other sent Will into another collision with the door frame. The house wouldn't survive a fight like this for long, and I needed to get my sister out before the ceiling came crashing down.

As I scooped her up, the bigger gargoyle took a swipe at me. Becks leapt at him first, climbing up onto his head and trying to scratch at his eyes. The gargoyle's claw missed, and I ducked underneath and ran into the bedroom. Shaking Becks off, the huge gargoyle launched himself at the door frame, teeth snapping, wings beating. Becks came streaking between his feet and turned back into human form. "I'll get Cori out."

"Thanks. I'll shift once you're out." I'd prefer for the others not to be in the house when I did so, but Will was resilient in his gargoyle form and I hadn't the faintest clue where the faerie even was.

As I tapped into the fire burning in my chest, the door frame buckled and the big gargoyle shouldered his way halfway into the bedroom.

"Shit." Becks recoiled from the window, and the two gargoyles now barring the way out. "How many of you fuckers are there?"

Too many. Trapped on both sides. It sure would have been nice if the half-faerie had let the rest of us in on that disappearing act of his.

The big gargoyle tore the door frame aside. Becks leaped at his face, scratching at his eyes, and I used the distraction to lift Cori onto my back, angling her body so that one of my hands was free. Red scales gleamed as my hand shifted to a claw, but I wasn't sure even my dragon claws could tear through a gargoyle's tough skin.

A crack split the window behind me. I dove behind the bed to shield Cori from the storm of broken glass and heard the gargoyle in the doorway snarling when a torrent of shards caught him full in the face. Shrieking noises followed, presumably him yelling at his buddy outside. Flat on the ground, I risked lifting my head to the window. The glass in the lower panes had shattered, and in the darkness, I glimpsed two winged figures diving at the ground. Or rather, at Astor. What the hell was he doing here?

The gargoyle in the bedroom doorway took another swipe at me and missed, his claw hitting the door frame again instead. Plaster crumbled, and the wall buckled from the impact. Alarm rang through me. At this rate they'd bring the whole ceiling down without me needing to shift into a dragon at all, and our sole exit route was occupied by two enraged gargoyles playing tag with an assassin.

Settling Cori on my back, I made for the shattered window. If Astor kept the gargoyles outside distracted, I might be able to run.

A blast from the living room shook the wall and took another chunk out of the plaster. The gargoyle in the doorway went flying, his wings caught in the blast, and a smaller gargoyle limped past him through the vacated doorway.

"Will," I said. "Let's go."

More glass showered the room, prompting me to back away from the window. Outside, I glimpsed one of the gargoyles kicking Astor down before grabbing the windowsill to climb in. As he lifted his curved claws, I stood over Cori, readied to fight until my last breath.

A flash of green light enveloped the room, and the ceiling came down in a crash of bricks and dust. I didn't even have time to close my eyes or scream, but the impact never came. Brick dust rained down as the ruin of the upper floor slid away as if an invisible shield lay above our heads. A shield made of dazzling green light.

The faerie reappeared beside the bed. He must have glamoured himself invisible, but that shield above our heads was no creation of glamour. We were encased in a semi-transparent bubble while the gargoyles in the living room took the full brunt of the collapsing ceiling, and the guy who'd been trapped in the doorway had vanished under a pile of plaster dust.

"Christ," gasped Will, who'd turned human again. He was bleeding badly from one leg, crimson soaking through his jeans. "Thanks, man," he added to the faerie, who didn't look up. Kit lay with his arms over his head, his pale skin shimmering with a similar greenish light to the barrier he'd conjured.

"Yeah… thanks." Becks was back in human form again, too, crouched breathlessly on all fours. "That was a close one."

"Tell me about it." I straightened upright, wary of making any sudden movements in case the spell protecting us broke, and nodded to Kit. "Thank you."

"Enough of the pleasantries," growled Astor through the back window. "Get out. Now."

I ignored him and checked Cori was breathing. Glad we'd retreated into the bedroom, where we kept our emergency packs, I reached under Cori's bed and hauled out my rucksack. Will did likewise and attempted to stand, but he was limping too much to walk in a straight line, let alone lift the half-faerie.

"I'll carry him," said Becks, noticing. "He's pretty lightweight."

Becks carried Kit out through the window first, while I

followed with Cori slung over my back. The two gargoyles who'd flown away would be back soon, once they knew we'd survived, and I was willing to bet that the ones we'd left in the house would dig their way out of the wreckage soon. They were resilient enough that even a house falling on them wouldn't slow them down for long.

"Another home bites the dust." Will climbed out slowly, gritting his teeth when his injured leg caught on the broken window frame. "What are we supposed to do now?"

"What else?" said Astor. "You don't have a choice. Your friends are injured, your sister is unprotected, and—"

"You don't need to tell me that," I snapped. "You know, if you've been keeping tabs on me the whole time, it'd be nice if you'd showed up *before* we got attacked rather than after for once."

"I hadn't a hope of overtaking the gargoyles in a car," said Astor. "I can take you to Giselle's place now. It's that or wait for the other gargoyles to come back and kill you, and that'd be a shame after I went to all this trouble."

"Oh, fine," I said. "Happy?"

"Ecstatic," he said. "Let's get out of here before one of you drops dead."

5

It wasn't an encouraging note to leave on. But the house was wrecked, a half-dozen gargoyles were out for our blood, and once again, I had to put my faith in someone who wasn't exactly known for being forthcoming with his own motives.

Astor's black vehicle wasn't the same car he'd driven before, but a large, comfortable unit with three rows of seats. Way too expensive for him to have purchased legally.

"You planned this, didn't you?" I asked, strapping Cori and Kit carefully into the back seat. The faerie whimpered but otherwise didn't speak. He probably wasn't a fan of cars, and being in a giant metal box wouldn't help the lingering effects of iron poisoning, but we could hardly leave him behind.

Will took over two thirds of the middle row with his bleeding leg, Becks squeezed in next to him, and I was left to take the front seat next to Astor.

"No," Astor said in answer to my question. "When I saw those gargoyles all flying towards your house at once, I followed them."

"And just happened to bring a king-sized car?"

"Guys!" said Will. "If any of you have a healing salve, it'd be appreciated, since I'm bleeding to death all over your seat."

Astor ground his teeth. "The car isn't mine, it's my work-place's. Can you be more careful?"

"I'll take it under advisement when I don't have a giant hole in my leg."

Astor started the engine. "We need to go. If those gargoyles come back, it'll be the worse for all of you."

"Hang on!" I grabbed my seat belt with one hand and dug in my rucksack with the other. Buckling myself in, I found our one remaining healing salve and passed it to Will.

"That's why you don't single-handedly take on two gargoyles at once," Becks said to him.

"I dropped a house on them," said Will. "You people have destroyed my pacifist tendencies. I blame the assassin."

Next to me, Astor's hands clenched over the wheel. "It may have escaped your attention that we're being followed."

Sure enough, I glanced in the side mirror and saw a winged shadow above the road. A second flew in behind.

"The gargoyles." My heart sank. "Drive."

"What do you think I'm doing?" Astor didn't pick up speed, nor did he look particularly concerned. Then again, League hunters were trained not to panic in even the direst situations. "They can't see inside the car."

"Yet." I sank lower in my seat, for all the good that would do. "Doesn't this fancy car have tinted windows?"

There was so little traffic around that we stood out a mile compared to the numerous ruined cars we passed at the roadside. With half the city difficult to drive through due to the debris left from the faeries' invasion, Astor's knowledge of the back roads would help us navigate faster, but it was no guarantee of escaping our overly persistent attackers.

"I'd thank you for rescuing us if not for your shit timing,"

Will said. "Ember's right. If you were following us around earlier today, why not warn us sooner?"

"I didn't know they'd show up at your house," he said. "Believe it or not, rescuing you from gargoyle mobs isn't my full-time occupation."

"Like you didn't follow Ember and Will to Magic Avenue?" Becks said. "You sent us there after this mythical Moonbeam and now we have gargoyles at our house thinking we killed one of their own. Was it you?"

"No, and we're in more trouble than I realised," Astor said tightly. "I heard about a witch's death—"

"When you went back to Magic Avenue to spy on us, I know." In the mirror, I saw gargoyles flying within our rear view, though they hadn't increased their speed. "The gargoyles cut Twill's throat and threw him in the river. Surprised we didn't take the blame for that one, too."

"So am I, since it seems a bad habit of yours." Astor sounded almost amused. "You do have a habit of attracting every source of trouble in London, don't you?"

"Ever since I met you," I corrected. "On top of that, we lost all the records we took from Twill's shop."

"You mean these?" Astor took one hand off the wheel and opened the compartment in front of me, handing me a piece of rolled-up paper.

I took it from him and unfurled the page. "When did you have time to grab this?"

"Let me see," Will demanded, leaning over the seat. "What does it say?"

"It's a list of potential buyers for artefacts that I assume he acquired illegally," Astor replied. "I imagine he was selling them to pay off his debts."

"And this is relevant because..." My gaze skimmed down the list of items and snagged on one word, scrawled near the bottom. "Because he had the Moonbeam."

There it was: crystal clear on the page. *Moonbeam.* And a list of buyers, but no confirmation of which, if any, he'd sold it to.

"If you got that from Twill's shop, are *you* the one who started the fire?" Will asked. "You should've told us. We'd have helped."

"No, we wouldn't have." I handed the document to Will over my shoulder. "You mean to say you walked into a burning building? On purpose?"

"Yes," Astor said shortly. "And no, it wasn't me who started it. But as soon as I saw the fire, I knew where to look."

"For proof that Twill handled the Moonbeam?" I queried. "You think someone was trying to hide the evidence?"

"He handled the Moonbeam three months ago," Will corrected. "According to the date on this paper. That was ages before he turned us in. There's no link to us."

"Except through the hunters." Had *they* taken the Moonbeam back? If so, that had surely been weeks ago, if not longer. Twill's killers might have had no idea he'd held it. But the timing of the blaze was no coincidence. "I wonder where he got it?"

"I couldn't begin to guess, but I found no records of him having sold it to anyone."

"Then someone stole it." I bolt upright when I saw that the winged shadow had moved much closer to the car. "Fuck. Astor, drive faster."

I immediately regretted my words when Astor took a sharp turn into a darkened street without any streetlamps and rattled over a series of potholes, tyres crunching with each jolt. A car had no hope of outracing a gargoyle when we had to contend with a maze of tight roads and the rubble of broken stones. I winced when we hit an obstacle so large that the car nearly went airborne.

"Okay, slow down!" I held on for dear life. "Or at least get us out of the dark before you puncture the tyres."

"Or drive straight into a swarm of redcaps," added Becks. "We have injured passengers, remember?"

"Yeah, I'm covered in blood," Will said. "I don't like the odds."

And Cori's in the back. I glanced at Astor, but the little I could see of his face showed an expression of absolute indifference.

"Seriously," I said. "Astor—"

"I'm doing my best to avoid getting us killed," he returned. "I could do without the running commentary."

I scowled at the dark street. Astor knew the city better than I did, but nothing in the vicinity remotely signalled 'safe hiding place'. I'd been assuming he'd meant to drive us to Giselle's house, but we'd have to lose our tail first. I held on tight as he swerved around a corner into a street flanked by dark buildings and littered with debris.

"Astor, this'll only slow us down, not them."

"We're nearly out."

The car's engine sputtered as he upped the speed again and we rattled over another unseen obstacle. Lucky it was too dark to tell if it was a piece of debris or a dead body lying discarded in the road.

My stomach swooped when we careened around another sharp turn, and a loud screech came from behind us as we emerged into sudden brightness. The street ahead was bathed in lamplight, the road clear from debris, and the houses spread out widely enough that we had ample room to manoeuvre.

"What are you playing at?" yelped Will from behind me. "This is mage territory."

So it was. The sudden lack of clutter on the road, coupled

with the large, expensive-looking houses on either side, left little doubt as to who was in charge here.

"See?" Astor fired a smirk at me. "Told you I'd lose them."

The car buckled as something heavy slammed down onto the roof. I yelled and slid down in my seat a moment before the ceiling sank inward where my face had been seconds before.

"Famous last words." I threw my arms over my head when the ceiling buckled again.

The car swerved to the side, almost crashing into one of the pristine gardens.

"The mages'll have their heads," said Becks, winding down the window behind me. Shifting into a cat, she climbed out as the car gave another shudder and the gargoyle's claw came down, piercing the glass on the windshield.

Astor swore explosively, swinging the wheel to avoid colliding with a low fence. There was little he could do to get rid of our unwanted passenger without losing control of the vehicle. The gargoyle crawled over the windshield, entirely blocking his view.

"Dammit." I slid my own window down, my claws ready. "Becks, get down from there!"

I could see her clinging to the gargoyle's head, biting and scratching, but his clawed feet refused to budge from the windshield.

I leaned out the window and swiped at the gargoyle's side, but Astor took another corner so abruptly that I nearly fell headfirst out into the street. From what I could tell from my half-upside-down state, we'd spun around and were headed back the way we came at breakneck pace. From the way my neck hurt, there was a real danger of that expression becoming literal, especially if we drove too close to a wall.

"Slow down!" I yelled over my shoulder.

Clinging onto the window one-handed, I managed to stab

the gargoyle's leg with my other claw. Blood gushed over the car's bonnet and side, and the stubborn bastard finally let go, his wings carrying him upward with Becks perched on his head.

"Get away from us," I snarled at the gargoyle. "Becks, get down!"

"Ember!" Astor shouted. "Get in here, *now*."

I threw myself back into the car as the side scraped along a brick wall. The motion landed me in Astor's lap, sprawling in an undignified heap.

"Are you trying to get us all killed?" I yelled up at his face.

"I'm trying to keep you alive," he yelled back. An ominous sputtering noise came from somewhere inside the car's bonnet, the wind roared past, and a high-pitched wail issued from the back and added to the general clamour. "And can you shut your friend up?"

"Kit saved our lives, arsehole. He doesn't deserve to die because of your shitty driving."

"I'd like to see you do the same." He swore when the car gave another shudder, and a bright flash ignited the sky.

"Becks, get back in here!" Will shouted from behind. "There's—"

The car juddered under the gargoyle's weight as a second bright flash reflected in the now-crooked mirror, accompanied by the rumble of thunder directly above the roof. Thunder and lightning. Not the ordinary kind.

Another supernatural was here.

"Becks!" Will leaned out of the window and caught her in his outstretched arms as a third bolt of lightning struck the road in front of the car. The weight on the roof lifted as the gargoyle took flight, while Astor gripped the steering wheel, guiding us down a side road between manor houses.

"Becks." I leaned forward, keeping one eye on the crooked

wing mirror and the other on the sky. "Are you okay back there?"

"I think so," Will answered. "She clawed me a little and she's covered in blood, but I don't think it's hers. Becks—*ow.* Put those claws away."

I could hear a faint moaning from the faerie in the back seat, but I couldn't see him from this angle. The front mirror had fallen off when the roof had half caved in, and Astor's wild driving had freaked me out almost as much as our airborne attacker. I craned my neck to see if we were still being followed, but the winged shadows had receded from sight.

"We've lost them," said Astor, following my field of vision. "They won't come after us again."

"Because you drove us into mage territory." Becks's voice was hoarse. "I swear, if you weren't at the wheel—"

"At least one of us would be dead," said Astor. "It was the only option, short of driving into the river. I didn't think you'd appreciate that."

No way, not when my baby sister was in the back seat. Didn't mean I wasn't pissed off with him for taking the initiative in such a bloody dangerous way.

"And we're going… where, exactly?" Will asked.

"Giselle's house."

Thought so. Giselle hadn't exactly given us a warm welcome the last time, though she'd grudgingly offered her help and I'd got the impression she was equally hostile to everyone who stopped by at her house on the outskirts of London. She and Astor had renounced the League around the same time, but while he'd pretended to remain loyal, she'd gone into hiding after escaping torture at Malkin's hands. The only people the League hated more than supernaturals were traitors, and her experiences had left her bitter, untrusting, and ill-disposed towards hunters and supernaturals alike.

And yet she might be the only person who had the information I wanted.

Astor gave me a sideways look. "You'll want to speak to her. It's important."

I loosened my grip on the seat as the car slowed down a fraction. "Yeah. I figured."

"Important how?" asked Will.

"It's not my place to tell you."

"She had the Moonbeam," I put in. "Right? She's the person who stole it from Malkin."

Astor didn't reply, which was answer enough.

"Wow," Becks said. "Sure would have been nice if you'd told us sooner."

"Yeah, it would have." I rubbed my sore neck. "I figured whoever stole it from the hunters must've got up close and personal with Malkin."

Her capture and torture at Malkin's hands was bound to be a sore subject with Giselle, but it couldn't be helped. Every conversation with Giselle was laced with barbed wire at the best of times.

Then again, I could say the same of Astor. I caught his eyes flicker towards me as he drove, but he didn't speak. Maybe he didn't want to say anything in front of the others, but I'd given him ample opportunities to come and find me alone and he hadn't said a word, not even to confirm he no longer wanted to stay in touch. It was the lack of closure that left me wrong-footed and kept me wondering if I might have taken the wrong step. Or if our mutual attraction meant nothing compared to the trainload of baggage we both brought to the table. Astor himself had said as much already.

I pretended to fall asleep against the window to lessen the awkward silence and tried not to think about Astor and his appalling sense of timing. When I did eventually doze off, I woke with my neck aching worse than ever. Astor had slowed the car, and when he came to a stop, the vehicle died with a slow moaning noise.

Astor swore colourfully and slammed a hand on the steering wheel. "This was my work car."

"You're the one who decided to try to outfox the gargoyles by taking us down a bunch of broken-down back alleys." I stretched out my neck and shoulders. "And since when did taxis look like miniature limousines?"

Astor shoved the door open and went to the back. Cori was strapped in next to Kit, and I reached for my sister. Astor tried to pick up Kit, but the faerie promptly started yelling incoherently.

"Shut up," snapped Astor. The faerie howled and squirmed, kicking his hands away.

"I don't think he likes you." I checked Cori was okay— mercifully, she hadn't taken any damage from our bumpy ride—and lifted her in my arms.

Will half fell out of the car, dragging his injured leg behind him, while Becks approached Astor. "Hand Kit over to me. He hates hunters."

"I'm not—" Astor's words were lost under another yell from the faerie. Resigned, he all but threw Kit at Becks. When she caught him, the faerie's yelling faded to a faint moaning.

Alone, Astor marched over to the house. The door lay half-open, and Giselle peered out, wearing the same worn dressing gown as she had during our last encounter.

"Don't you look like a heap of shit," she said. "What did you do to the car?"

"Long story," said Astor, pushing past her into the house.

Giselle rolled her eyes and limped inside, too. She'd

broken her leg at some point during her imprisonment at the hunters' hands, and had probably never seen a doctor.

I carried Cori inside, and Becks and Will trailed after me. The living room was set out the same way as before, with mattresses and sleeping bags littering almost every inch of the floor, a small kitchen at the back, and a bedroom through another door that Giselle had claimed for herself.

I found a spare mattress and lowered Cori onto it, then took off my rucksack. To my relief, my possessions had survived our hair-raising drive, including the potions we needed to keep Cori hydrated while she was unconscious. Otherwise, we'd been forced to leave most of our supplies behind.

"Great." Becks put the faerie down on another mattress. "We're really in the shit this time. No jobs, no homes, and a flock of gargoyles out for our blood."

"What the devil is that?" asked Giselle, eyeing the semi-conscious half-faerie.

"His name's Kit," I replied. "He doesn't talk much."

"Nobody said anything about faeries." Giselle gave Astor an accusing look.

He offered a flat stare in return. "You never asked."

"I'm not keeping a faerie here."

"He saved our lives." It seemed a poor repayment to bring him to a place littered with so many reminders of the torture he'd suffered, but there were few hospitals willing to treat half-faeries at all, let alone ones who knew about the effects of iron poisoning. "He was Malkin's personal prisoner in the Stronghold."

Giselle's mouth tightened. "Fine, but if he does anything to draw the fae into my house, he's gone. I haven't survived two years here by offering shelter to every supernatural in who comes to my doorstep."

"Aren't we the first supernaturals you've let in?" asked

Will. "If you're planning to screw us over, please get it over with. We'd appreciate the heads-up."

"I'm not planning to," said Giselle. "You did us all a favour when you destroyed the Stronghold and forced Malkin to abandon his house. That's the only reason I'm letting you and your friends in here. Don't make me regret it."

"All right." It wasn't like we had much choice. Will's house at Magic Avenue was the only one of our shelters in a semi-decent condition, and the fire at Twill's house was a glaring reminder that someone very much wanted us to never return.

Kit mumbled something under his breath and his eyelids flickered, but he seemed as unaware of his surroundings as ever. I had no more idea how to help him than I did my sister, and I already wondered if we'd made a mistake in leaving the city.

This is where we needed to be, I reminded myself. Giselle had stolen the Moonbeam. She'd know if we could use it to save Cori—and if the hunters had indeed been the ones responsible for stealing it back.

6

Even after all the turmoil of the previous day, I found it difficult to rest. I admitted defeat in the early hours of the morning, as the first rays of dawn light poked through gaps in the threadbare curtain. Becks and Will were both passed out on mattresses, the latter surrounded by several half-made spells he'd pulled out of his rucksack the previous night. Cori and Kit occupied one corner, and the half-faerie's faint moaning was the only sound in the silent house. Giselle must be in her room, so where was Astor? Maybe he'd gone out again, but the car had taken a beating, and it was lucky the fancy vehicle had made it here in one piece.

Where'd he get that thing? I thought back to that sense of familiarity when I'd first set eyes on it, and then our abrupt detour through mage territory. He'd claimed the car belonged to his workplace. He'd also told me he was a taxi driver. He might be lying, but the mages had cars like that, and if he worked for *them*, it explained why he'd felt confident driving through their territory. That or he'd stolen it, but I had a hard time imagining him going out of his way to earn the ire of the one group of supernaturals who might have a chance in hell of besting the Orion League.

Or not. Malkin's plan to gain power would involve removing the Mage Lords from their current position as the leaders of the supernatural community by necessity, and the overblown speech he'd given prior to our breaking into the Orion Stronghold had hinted that he intended to make a move soon. I'd thought the League had avoided an all-out attack on the Mage Lords due to knowing they'd be outclassed, but in retrospect, it made sense that Malkin had been playing a long game. The mages represented what every hunter hated—the notion of the supernaturals being in charge of society—and only their wealth and privilege had sheltered them from being the hunters' immediate targets.

Why, then, had Astor decided to play chauffeur for them? They wouldn't treat him kindly if they learned he'd once worked for the League, and Astor himself regarded the mages with disdain at best, as far as I knew.

Right. I was wide awake now, and if Astor wasn't in the downstairs flat, he must be upstairs. Or in Giselle's room, but I doubted it. The pair had more of a sibling dynamic than a romantic one.

I tiptoed into the corridor and up the narrow staircase. I hadn't been upstairs before, but a partly opened door revealed a large room that mirrored the one of the floor below, with bare floorboards covered in sleeping bags and mattresses and weapons piled in the corner.

Astor lay on a bare mattress next to the window. He'd removed his jacket and wore a thin white T-shirt that revealed the tattoo lines on his arms and chest. I averted my eyes, flushing. *Come on. You're angry with him.*

Waking up an assassin was generally a terrible idea, but I'd run out of patience. I strode over, and his hand shot out, locking around my leg and pulling me down. I tried to aim for the mattress and instead landed face-first on top of him. My forehead cracked off the bare floorboards, and a starburst of lights danced before my eyes.

"Ow." I groaned, rubbing my forehead. "I think you gave me a concussion."

"You gave yourself one." His chest moved when he spoke, his voice vibrating through my body and causing my shifter side to stir with interest.

"What's going on?" a sleepy voice called upstairs, followed by footsteps.

"Ah." I pushed off Astor, but he sat up abruptly at the same time and caused me to fall flat on my face again. This time I landed splayed across his legs, my nose to the wooden floor. "You did that on purpose, arsehole."

Will peered into the room. "Oh, for pity's sake. Shut the door if you're going to molest one another."

"Trust me, that's the opposite of what's going on here," I growled at the floorboards. "He's a bastard."

"Tell me something I don't know, little dragon," said Astor.

I climbed off him, and this time he behaved himself. *Honestly.* Was he so reluctant to talk to me that he'd rather I knocked myself out cold?

"What's going on?" asked Becks from the landing. "Is someone being murdered?"

"Nope." I rubbed my forehead, side-eyeing Astor as he rose to his feet. "Before you can sneak off, when did you plan to tell us you're using a car that belongs to the mages?"

"What?" said Becks, at the same time as Will said, "I knew it looked familiar."

"That's what I just realised," I added. "An interesting choice of transport for someone who'd be locked in one of their cells if they ever got wind that he used to work for the League."

Astor's expression was a blank slate. "I have a solid alias. The mages are always looking for drivers, and it's a convenient way to get around the city without drawing undue attention."

"It's also a good way to get gossip." Will gave him an assessing look. "Is this where you hear your rumours?"

Oh. I looked at Astor. "Did you hear the *mages* mention the Moonbeam?"

His jaw worked. "Yes, but only as a legend. Unfortunately, the mages don't have it, and I gather that most of them think it's been missing for years if they believe it exists at all. They don't know the League had it."

"And Giselle stole it." I spoke in a low voice. "We need to ask her for the details."

"I'd suggest leaving that to me," said Astor. "She won't know who currently has it, or their intentions, but it's somewhere to start."

"What are you all whispering about?" Giselle herself came limping into the room. Only an Elite hunter could climb stairs that silently. I should have figured she'd heard the ruckus.

"The Moonbeam." I ignored Astor's warning look. "We need to know everything about it."

Giselle's face blanked as effectively as Astor's had. "I see."

"Surely he told you we need it." I jerked my chin at him. "And why. My sister is in a coma, and Astor claims that the Moonbeam is the only way to wake her up."

"It's true," Astor said.

"Ah." Giselle shook her head. "Then I'm sorry, but there's nothing I can do."

"We're not asking for help, just information," I said, undeterred. "You stole the Moonbeam from Malkin, right? That's why he locked you up and tortured you?"

Giselle gave a rasping laugh. "You have quite the knack

for getting straight to the point, don't you? No, I stole it after my escape. I'd known he left certain valuables in his house that he wouldn't have had time to move to the Stronghold when the faeries invaded."

"Why'd steal that one?" Becks wanted to know. "I mean, what use would you have for a magical artefact that boosts shifters' powers and cures them of illness?"

"I needed cash to make my escape, sweetheart," said Giselle. "The Moonbeam is unique even for a magical arte-fact. You might recognise the name given to those leaves the League is so fond of using to lure shifters into their clutches. From what I gathered from Malkin, the Moonbeam suppresses a shifter's human side until the beast is all that's left."

My mind flickered back to those wolves the League used to guard the jail. Was that how they'd turned them into murderous killing machines who didn't recognise their fellow shifters? "Malkin wanted to use it to control us?"

"He wanted a ready-made weapon," she corrected. "To my knowledge, there's no limit to the number of shifters the Moonbeam can draw under its spell. If they get their hands on it again, the League will be more than a match for the mages."

"Maybe they already have it."

A ripple of emotion passed over Giselle's face, too fast for me to grasp. "I would prefer to hope that isn't the case, sweetheart, or else your personal interests will be the least of your problems."

"Personal interests?" I echoed. "I already risked my neck in the Stronghold to save my sister. I'm not giving up on her now."

"What did you expect to happen after you sold it?" Becks said to Giselle. "Did you think the League would let it go?"

"I sold it to a dealer who agreed to keep it off the market," she said. "A witch, of course. I knew an object like that would wreak havoc among the shifters."

"How generous of you." I gave an eye-roll. "Well, the last record shows it was in the hands of a shady witch who had debts to a local gargoyle gang. Bad enough debts that he sold his own neighbours out to the hunters."

"And now you've brought the same gang to my doorstep." Giselle coughed. "I suppose I deserve as much for keeping my doors open to strangers."

"You sold the bloody thing," I growled. "What did you expect? Also, the gargoyles didn't follow us past mage territory, and the hunters were looking for you anyway. You told us yourself."

"Gargoyles." Giselle grunted. "If anything, I'm surprised *they* haven't stolen it. They cropped up in every bad story I heard about supernaturals in London."

"Really." Will gave her a look free of his usual cheer. He was usually open to joking about his fellow gargoyles, but not when those remarks came from an outsider. "There's one gang responsible for ninety percent of the trouble. They call themselves the Fanged, and they pretty much own the supernatural underworld. A lot of shifters tried to get help from them during the invasion. Protection against the faeries, you know."

"In other words, they're the sort of people who'd want the Moonbeam." Had Twill got the Moonbeam from them, or had they found out he'd had it in his possession? Either might explain why they'd dumped his body in the river, but the gargoyles who'd cornered us at our house hadn't mentioned the Moonbeam. "I can't decide if I'd rather they were the ones who had it or the hunters."

"Oh, I'd take the hunters," Will said to my surprise. When everyone looked at him, he shrugged. "My dad used to be a member of the Fanged himself, but they don't tend to look kindly on shifters who get too friendly with the witches. That's how I knew I wanted nothing to do with them even if the faeries beat down my doors."

I stared at him. I'd known his dad had died when he was a baby, but not that his fellow gargoyles had been involved. "Seriously? You don't think they *do* have the Moonbeam, do you?"

"The ones who attacked your house last night were in human form before they shifted," Astor put in. "They can't have been that strongly under the Moonbeam's effects, or else they wouldn't even have been able to use human speech."

"Like you'd know," said Becks, who'd looked outraged at Will's revelation. "Twill was a fucking idiot for thinking selling shifters to the hunters to pay off his debts wouldn't get his own throat cut."

"The question is whether he sold the Moonbeam to the hunters willingly or if they stole it," I added. "Given that he still owed the gargoyles money three months later, I'm betting on the latter."

"Yeah, we need more information," Will said. "Tell you what, I can ask around Magic Avenue if he was burgled three months ago. Nobody's going to think that's a strange question."

"Except there are gargoyles waiting to ambush you as soon as you go back to London," Astor added.

"Even the Fanged can't watch the streets and the skies at the same time," Will said. "What else are we supposed to do out here?"

"Except ruin my peace and quiet?" Giselle took a decisive step back. "You're free to do as you will as long as you don't draw your enemies here. Now, if you're done trying to murder one another, I'm going back to bed."

"*Are* we done trying to murder each other?" Astor's

mouth tilted up in a smile that somehow made me even more furious. "You tell me, little dragon."

"This isn't a fucking joke," I said through clenched teeth. "We're fugitives, and now we can't even work as mercenaries without telling the whole world we're shifters because some bright spark decided they needed the name and address of every employee on record."

Astor lifted a brow. "Since when?"

"Since yesterday." I glared at him. "Did the mages discuss *that* while you were spying on them?"

"No. Why would they?"

"Because they're the ones in charge?" I pointed out. "Whoever told old Harwood and the other mercenary organisations in north London to keep a list of their employees' information must have had some serious clout. They told me to apply for ID, which would instantly out me as supernatural."

"The mages aren't in regular contact with the human mercenary units," said Astor. "I'm fairly sure they voted against a registry of supernaturals when the subject came up years ago, actually."

Huh. That didn't necessarily mean the mages had wanted to do us a favour. After all, if someone assembled a registry of everyone magical in London, their own names would end up on the same list. I didn't see most supernaturals going in for that, even the ones at the top of the pyramid.

"Do they want a medal?" Will retreated from the room. "I'm going to see how many of my spells survived our trip in the car."

"I'll help." Becks joined him, a clear indication that she intended to leave Astor and me to talk alone. And while that was exactly what I'd wanted to do earlier, I really wasn't in the mood to deal with more of his mind games.

"And me." I tried to catch his eye, but he'd turned to the

window, watching the lightening sky. "Let me know if you remember anything else your employers might have said."

Astor, of course, didn't take the bait. Irritated with myself, I went downstairs and found Will sorting through a pile of spells shaped like wristbands and short sticks.

"I didn't know you had more explosives," Becks commented.

"A handful," Will said. "We're low on healing spells, but I did fetch some more ingredients from the shop yesterday on my way back from following that gargoyle. I was hoping taking a detour would mean nobody tailed me, but apparently not."

From the corner, the faerie uttered a shrill wail, prompting Giselle to bang on the bedroom wall.

Becks sank onto a mattress. "You know, Giselle sort of has a point. What if the half-faerie *does* draw attention? Not from the hunters, but the fae can sense each other in ways we don't even know about."

"I know." I chewed the inside of my cheek. "We need to figure out a way to help him *and* Cori, but unless someone knows how to cure a faerie from the aftereffects of iron poisoning, I'm clueless."

"Yeah, me too," said Becks. "Same goes for finding the Moonbeam, to be honest. It might have been literally anywhere for the last three months. It's not like we're deep in the supernatural underworld. If we were, we'd probably be floating in the river like that gargoyle by now."

"Yeah, no thanks." A shudder travelled through Will's shoulders. "Seeing as I'm the only one of us who can fly without turning into a giant red dragon, I'll use a shadow spell and head back into the city to poke around."

"No," said Becks and I at the same time.

"Not through gargoyle territory," I added. "It's too risky.

They know you by sight in both human and gargoyle forms, remember?"

"Aren't you cheerful today?" Will rolled his eyes. "They can't see through shadow spells, remember? I'll only be gone for an hour. If I'm not back after that, I don't know, I'll send up a smoke signal."

"Remember when phones actually worked?" Becks said in reminiscent tones. Most of the mobile phones we'd owned had either broken or been abandoned when we'd left our hideouts, and we'd come to a mutual agreement not to give the League any more ways to track us down. The notion of Malkin using a method as mundane as ordinary human technology to corner us struck me as unlikely, but you never knew.

"Use mine," said Giselle from the bedroom doorway. "I have a box of stolen electronics, and the signal out here isn't half bad."

"Wait, really?" I swivelled to her, frowning. "Burner phones, are they?"

"What else?"

Giselle limped back into her bedroom. Returning, she threw one phone at me and the other at Will. I caught mine by my fingertips, but the second phone flew past Will and landed on the mattress.

He picked it up, examining the screen. "Is the internet working on this thing?"

"Rarely," she said. "Why?"

Will poked the touchscreen with a finger. "Just trying to think of alternative ways to track the Moonbeam down. There used to be a whole secret online network for supernaturals."

"Aha," Giselle said, inexplicably. "I knew it."

"Knew what?" asked Becks.

"Astor owes me now," she said with a touch of smugness. "We had a bet on that the supernaturals had their own secret dark corner of the internet."

"Of course we did," I said. "How do you think we kept ourselves safe from the hunters, pre-invasion?" I clamped my mouth shut, annoyed with myself for forgetting I was talking to someone who barely qualified as an ally. "Anyway, Will, if you need urgent help, message us and I'll fly in." Not ideal, but walking would take too long and I'd long since abandoned any hope of keeping my dragon side in check.

"You can always borrow the car," said Giselle. "If it's driveable in its current state."

"Probably not," I said. "Also, none of us can drive."

"Of course you can't." Disdain dripped from her voice. "Londoners."

"We don't even have birth certificates or passports, let alone driving licences," I said. "For obvious reasons. Sorry if that's not good enough for you."

"Also, I'm short-sighted and lost my glasses two years ago, so you really don't want me behind the wheel," added Becks.

"You're all a mess, aren't you?" asked Giselle.

"Speak for yourself," Becks retaliated. "At least I don't spend my time squatting in a hovel full of junk, bitching at anyone who tries to show me compassion."

Giselle cut her a stare. "I can still put a knife through your eye from a hundred feet away."

"Also, we *are* a mess," Will said placatingly. "But we have a spectacular track record for getting out of shitty situations. I'll ask if Twill was robbed three months ago. Anything else?"

"If you ask about the Moonbeam, the witches might not necessarily know of it by name." I turned to Giselle. "What exactly does it look like?"

"It's a rock, about this big." She measured between her

fingers. "The size of my palm. It's jet black in colour, but glows when there are shifters nearby. That's how I knew which areas to avoid when I was on the run."

My skin prickled. "What do you mean by that?"

"She means their hunting wolves." Becks growled. "Right?"

Giselle didn't so much as blink under the heated glares of three shifters. "Yes. They're under orders to kill intruders on sight."

"Were those orders given by someone using the Moonbeam?" My nails bit into my palms. "Yeah, if Malkin has it, we're getting it back."

Giselle gave a soft snort. "You're beyond foolish to waste the chance you won when you escaped the Stronghold. Malkin barely had the chance to start on you, and if you think I'm broken, you haven't seen anything yet."

"He put my sister into a coma," I said. "He tried to force me to murder the only other living dragon shifter I've met. He tortured *children*. I've seen plenty, and if he burned away all your humanity and not mine, that's your problem to bear."

Giselle's eyes narrowed. "You're lucky Astor ordered me to take you in, but he never said you and your friends could stay here indefinitely. And you'd be unwise to forget what we are. Astor might be looking to make up for what he did. I never said I was."

She hobbled back to her room and slammed the door behind her. We watched for a wary moment, half expecting her to come out with a gun and shoot at us, but she didn't return.

Becks took Giselle's place on the sofa. "Never thought I'd say this, but I'd rather spend time around your hunter than her."

"He's not mine," I muttered. "Believe me, this situation is less than ideal for everyone involved."

The faerie wailed in his sleep, beating at the mattress with his fists.

"Me, too, mate," I said. "Me, too."

7

W ill returned within the hour. A good job, because I'd chewed my nails to ribbons by that point and would likely have got myself kicked out of Giselle's house if she'd left her room or spoken a word to us since our argument earlier. Astor hadn't shown himself either, and Becks had shifted into a cat and climbed out a window to avoid 'being trapped in the same room as someone as tetchy as a chimera caught in a net', as Will put it. Kind of unfair, if you asked me.

After I'd worn holes in my socks from pacing the floor, I planted myself next to Cori's mattress and told her about the Moonbeam. I talked to her every day, if I could, though I didn't know if she could hear me in her comatose state, and the past day had given me a long list of updates. It was hard not to dissolve into a rant about Astor's infuriating behaviour and Giselle's general attitude problem, so when I reached the end of the updates, I pulled out the notebook and read her some of that instead. I'd pretty much memorised the bits written in English after years of scouring every word for clues about my fellow dragon shifters, though the section written in another language was as inscrutable as ever.

A memory nudged at me of a piece of paper I'd seen in the Stronghold. I'd been certain the writing had been the same, but I'd been too intent on escape to pick it up and look closer. I was sure it had been inside the faerie's prison cell, but I didn't want to wake him and ask, so I returned to pacing until a fluttering noise outside the window heralded Will's return.

Becks meowed from the windowsill, and I ran to the door to join her. Will landed in the front garden, feathers sticking up in all directions and the distinct smell of smoke hanging over him. He turned human again, coughing a couple of times.

Becks shifted into human form, too. "Any signs of the Moonbeam?"

"Another gargoyle died," Will said hoarsely. "On the docks. Police everywhere—the human ones, that is, but I bet the mages will be sniffing around soon."

A chill slid down my spine. "Another one?"

"Yeah." Will coughed again as he followed us through the door. "It looks like he was killed in mid-air and crash-landed by the river."

"Who did it, another gargoyle?" I entered the living room, unease stirring inside me. One group of supernaturals being targeted by an unknown killer usually meant usually bad news for the rest of us.

"No clue. My shadow spell was wearing off by then, so I went into Magic Avenue to buy some more ingredients."

"For what?" Becks asked. "I thought you were supposed to be looking out for the Moonbeam."

"Nobody in the Avenue has heard of it," said Will. "But I did get some tips on how to brew up a spell to counter iron poisoning."

I looked at the faerie, who stirred restlessly in the corner. "You did?"

"Yeah. Would've cost an arm and a leg to get the ingredients if Keira hadn't been willing to accept a favour in exchange. I owe her for this, but the poor guy doesn't seem to be getting any better without help."

"Yeah." My chest tightened. "Wish we could do the same for Cori."

"That's the bad news. The other bad news," Will amended. "There doesn't seem to be a cure for whatever's wrong with her. I'm inclined to believe the assassin told the truth. Keira is one of the most knowledgeable people I've met, and she said most sleeping potions have little effect on shifters. The League must have modified theirs especially."

"Figures." I hadn't held out much hope of finding a witch-made cure, but my heart dipped all the same. "Astor had no reason to lie, though."

"Also, his car's gone," Will added. "I saw."

"He must have climbed out the window." So much for him telling us what he was up to. Aside from playing chauffeur for the mages. "Probably took it to the garage. It's hardly in any fit state to be used as a taxi."

He might be out of a job soon, though it was beyond me to guess *why* he'd chosen such a risky mode of employment. The pay might be enough to make up for the inherent danger, but I doubted the mages would have any interest in looking for the Moonbeam, and if they did, they'd want it for their own possession, not ours.

"That leaves us with no way back to London," I murmured. "We really need a new hideout that's not out in the middle of nowhere."

"You know, I never invited you here." Giselle poked her head out of her bedroom. "I'd be more than happy to kick you out if you need an incentive to leave."

"That's not what I meant." I should have figured she'd be listening in. "Did you know Astor took off?"

She closed the door again in answer.

Will blew out a breath. "I almost wish I'd stayed in London."

"And I wish I'd come." Sitting still and twiddling my thumbs wasn't my style, and with Astor gone, I had even less reason to stick around. "How about we go back later after we put together some more shadow spells?"

"You mean after *I* make some more shadow spells," Will said, but in a good-natured way. "That was the plan, but I'll have to leave the anti-iron poisoning potion brewing while we're gone. And we'll have to avoid the Avenue. I exhausted all my leads already and people'll start to get suspicious if I keep showing up and asking weird questions."

"You really didn't learn anything new?"

He shook his head. "You know Twill. The tight-lipped bastard would never have admitted to his neighbours that someone broke in and robbed him, and they must have been stealthy enough not to be spotted."

"Sounds like the hunters." I thought. "Maybe we can track down whoever Twill bought the Moonbeam from in the first place."

"We can try." Will lifted a pile of ingredients and carried them into the kitchen. "Now, you two make yourselves useful and help me with these."

An hour and a quick meal later, we had three freshly brewed shadow spells at the ready. I settled onto Will's gargoyle back with Becks perched on my shoulder. It wasn't particularly comfortable for any of us, but with Astor still absent, we had no other way into the city. I didn't like leaving Cori or Kit either, but with Giselle unwilling to leave her room, I reasoned that there was little chance of her throwing the half-faerie out on the streets while we were gone.

Will flew up into the low-hanging clouds, which kept us hidden from people on the ground but also resulted in us being drenched in the fine drizzle lingering in the air. Gargoyles didn't mind getting wet, but Becks hissed and dug her claws into my leg, while I ducked my head in a futile attempt to keep my face dry.

Soon London unfolded beneath us, the ribbon-shape of the Thames winding amongst the buildings. From this height, the city resembled its old self, pre-invasion. Only the significantly wider patches of green where faeries' magic had hit and caused the wild plants and trees to grow excessively hinted at the sudden increase in magic in this realm. The urban sprawl remained the same as ever, and it wasn't until we dipped below the clouds that the open destruction became apparent. Shells of ruined apartment blocks and office buildings speared the sky, and a winged shadow rose upward from one of those buildings. *Ah, shit.*

Will flew higher into the clouds, prompting a yelp from Becks as we were both drenched in rainwater. I gritted my teeth and held my breath, shuddering as droplets of water slid down the back of my jacket and pooled at the base of my spine.

A few tense seconds passed before Will flew out of the clouds. The gargoyle had gone, but when we descended over central London, I spied the flicker of flames somewhere near Charing Cross. *Crap. That's Magic Avenue.*

The blaze had drawn a crowd, and we had fly around Trafalgar Square to avoid a cluster of emergency services vehicles on our descent. The smell of burning was thick in the air, mingling with the drizzle as we landed in an alleyway just outside Magic Avenue.

Becks hopped off me and turned into her human form, giving herself a vigorous shake to dislodge the raindrops from her hair. "Never again," she said. "I could hardly breathe up there."

"I think you clawed a hole in my leg." I climbed off Will's back, too. "What now?"

"Put the shadow spells on," Will said. "I'll find out what's going on."

"You're the one the gargoyles are after," I reminded him.

"They aren't here," said Will. "And Ember, did you forget you turned into a dragon in public?"

"I don't need a shadow spell," Becks said. "Nobody ever pays cats any attention."

"If you're sure." I reached up my sleeve for the band-shaped shadow spell, which had slid halfway up my arm while we'd been flying, and tugged it back down. "But if the gargoyles come back, we're getting the hell out."

We entered the Avenue to find half the street had come out to view the blaze. A middle-aged woman with dark hair streaked with grey stood outside the burning house with a livid expression that made it plain that it was her property that had been targeted.

"Hey," said Will to her. "What's going on? How did this happen?"

She turned accusing eyes onto him. "How else? You and your friends. I suppose you think it's funny."

"What are you talking about?" asked Will, echoing my thoughts. "We had nothing to do with this."

She grunted. "First your dragon friend makes a public spectacle of herself and now this. Do you think I'm dense?"

Oh, damn. Not all of Magic Avenue's residents had seen me shift, but some had, and if they'd caught sight of the newspapers afterwards, they'd have also read the bullshit accusations of property damage that Malkin had planted in there. You'd think that it would have occurred to her that everyone outside on the street would have seen a dragon fly in and set her house on fire, but apparently not.

"No." Will eyed her in bewilderment. "I just got here and wondered what happened."

"Shifters happened," called a man from across the street. "You're a menace. Slaughtering one another left and right and terrorising us ordinary citizens. No wonder they want us all on a register so they can weed out the troublemakers."

"Hey, we're supposed to be on the same side." Will raised his hands in a placating manner. "What do you mean by register?"

"The letter that showed up this morning, what else?" said the witch. "We all got one. Didn't you?"

"I haven't been here."

Will ducked as a whistling sounded and a small projectile hit the pavement inches away, thrown from a nearby window. A cloud of smoke burst out, along with a shower of sparks. I broke into a run, Becks streaking past me in cat form. Will followed at a sprint until we'd rounded the Avenue's corner and left the witches behind.

"Damn." I rubbed smoke from my eyes. "That was a nasty piece of work. What was their problem?"

"Shifters being blamed for shit they didn't do, same as usual." Becks reappeared in human form, her arms folded over her chest. "And what the hell was all that about a register?"

"Someone's compiling a list of shifters?" Will guessed. "Yeah, I don't buy that it's anything official."

"I bet it's the same people who stole the Moonbeam," said Becks. "Maybe they're trying to get us killed by the local gargoyles so they don't have to bother themselves."

"I'd have thought the League would have gone for a more overt approach." I didn't see them making friends with gargoyle street gangs, either. "But you're right that this isn't likely to be a request from the normal authorities. The mages wouldn't have a reason to have us all on record."

"No, but the hunters didn't need a list to find us the first time around," said Will. "I don't see how this will help them at all."

"Unless they're expanding," said Becks darkly. "And finding more victims to use that Moonbeam on."

"Exactly." I'd feared as much myself. "I think we should head back to Harwood's office. I know *he* won't have a clue if the hunters have the Moonbeam or not, but he might at least know who gave the order." And if he didn't share that information willingly, I was more than happy to employ my claws as an incentive.

"I don't like it," said Becks. "Don't get me wrong, I wouldn't mind spilling a little more hunter blood, but we don't know nearly enough about what they're up to. We don't need to walk straight into another trap."

"Exactly." Will nodded. "We've played into their hands entirely too many times, and this time we have a bunch of gargoyles chasing us as well as the League waiting to pounce on us from wherever they're hiding. I don't like the odds."

"Nor me, but I think it's worth poking around at our old workplace," I said. "Harwood won't have locked up the place. It'll be easy to get in."

"Yeah, I can sneak into his office," said Becks. "I still think it's a bad idea, but we don't have any ties in that area anymore. It's not like they can destroy our house twice."

"True," Will relented. "All right, let's go and poke around the mercenary office and hope the Fanged aren't waiting behind Harwood's desk."

"Nah, they won't want to put their names on a list." That much I knew.

Will shifted again, and I climbed onto his back, while Becks hid inside my coat this time. I didn't like travelling this way even under a shadow spell, but at least it was faster than using the tunnels.

Soon, we landed in a deserted street near to the mercenary unit where we'd worked until the previous day. The office was in the same condition we'd left it in, down to the misspelled plaque next to the door.

As we neared the front, a low growl sounded. Then a giant beast covered in fur came out from behind the building, stalking towards us with murder in its eyes.

8

Whoa. I leaped back as the beast's teeth snapped inches from where I'd been standing. Alarm froze me for a moment, both from the sudden shock of the attack and the fact that it'd found me when I was hidden by a shadow spell. Shifters had a far better sense of smell than humans did, but I didn't know if the beast was a shifter or some kind of fae instead. Shaggy black fur covered its body, making it look somewhere between a bear and a dog.

The beast roared, displaying rows of sharp teeth, and swiped with one giant paw. Becks ran underneath, circling its legs in the way she usually did to bring a larger opponent crashing to its knees, while Will approached warily from the air. Even with his wings spread, his gargoyle form was far smaller than the beast.

I twisted the shadow spell on my wrist to switch it off—I might need to use it later—and let my claws slide out. "Who are you?"

The beast roared in response, bloodlust gleaming in its

eyes. I'd seen shifters in a frenzy before, but it was a long way from sunset and I didn't think the full moon was due for another week at least.

"Are you a shifter?" I raised my claws in warning. "Or are you a faerie?"

The beast growled and swiped with both paws. Will took flight to avoid taking a blow to the face. I caught the second hit in my claw, but the impact still sent me staggering back. The beast was strong even by shifter standards, and there was no telling how much damage it might do if we let it roam free in the area. As far as I knew, mostly humans lived around here, and the shifter had caused enough of a ruckus that curious passersby would show up soon enough.

"Stop!" I pushed against its splayed paw, but the beast refused to yield, nor did it budge an inch.

Becks prowled around, clawing at its legs, to no avail. Without warning, the shifter ripped its paw out of my grip, rearing up on its hind legs. I had no time to brace myself before my feet left the ground and I flew a good ten feet into a garden wall. An overgrown bush broke my fall, but all the air rushed out of my lungs as my back and shoulders screamed in protest. Will and Becks both shouted my name.

Fuck, that hurt. Head pounding, I turned back towards the fight as the beast flung Will into the doorway to the mercenary office.

"Will!" I yelled.

A scent overpowered my senses, flooding my nostrils and igniting the fire inside me. The source lay scattered on the guild's doorstep. *Moonbeam leaves.*

Someone had left bait here. They'd wanted to draw the shifter's attention directly to the mercenaries' doorstep.

Will staggered away from the door, still in gargoyle form, but he didn't look to be seriously hurt. Becks continued to weave in and out of the beast's legs, nipping and scratching, but her wildcat claws couldn't do much damage to a creature that size. The beast's paw caught Becks, throwing her into the air. Will took flight at once and caught her before she hit the ground.

I approached the beast for a renewed attack and aimed at its leg, hoping to slow it down. My claws sank through fur and flesh, and the creature bellowed in rage, kicking at me. I dodged the blow and yanked my claws from its flesh, thick blood spilling out onto the road.

I jumped aside as it reared back again. Above, Will suddenly stopped in mid-air, his gaze fixed on the beast. Becks slid from his slack grip, plummeting towards the ground. I lunged to catch her in my outstretched arms. Becks's claws dug in, but rather than wriggling free as she normally would, she remained frozen, her eyes fixed on the beast just like Will's.

Oh, hell. Had the shifter used some kind of spell on them? I'd seen something similar in the invasion, but only used by the fae against humans. Not from one shifter against others.

The smell of moonbeam leaves seemed to intensify, and scales spread up my lower arms to my elbows and then higher. I'd have to fully shift to stand a chance of bringing my opponent to heel single-handedly.

As the beast prowled towards me, I held Becks protectively and stared into its eyes, willing it to return to reason. "I don't want to hurt you."

My words had no effect. Becks slid from my grip as I was once again flung into the air.

Before I hit the ground, I let the fire overflow, spreading down my legs in the form of bright-red scales. My shoulders bunched, my head elongating and wings spreading from my shoulder blades. I landed on my feet, grappling with the oncoming fire threatening to consume everything I was, readied to burn straight through my enemy.

No. Don't. I reined the flames in and fought with claws and teeth instead, locking together with the beast in a violent grapple.

The shifter roared loud enough to shake the buildings, and I roared louder. Wrenching free, I tore into its body, my nose filled with the scent of blood and fire.

At once it ceased struggling, the pounding of its heartbeat fading as Will's cry of warning broke through the static in my ears. At the street's end, the first onlookers had begun to arrive, pointing and staring at our group. Or rather, at me.

Will grabbed Becks and pulled her onto his back. I took flight when he did, moving without conscious command, my mind split between human and dragon. Below, the beast lay dead, its blood staining my claws. The smell of moonbeam leaves pursued me into the sky, as if to remind me of the trap the hunters had laid. Had they hoped the shifter would kill us or had the mercenaries been the targets instead? Nobody had even been inside the guild, including Harwood. There were too many humans present for the hunters to show their faces in person. The sound of a police's siren reached me, but I kept flying, faster than I ever had before.

The city became a blur beneath me. I beat my wings until my whole body ached. A nagging reminder in the back of my mind told me that I was unaccustomed to using the muscles I didn't have in my human form and that pushing my body to its limits would only slow my recovery, but I kept going, as though if I pumped my wings fast enough, I could shake loose my memories of the fight and forget how I'd killed one of my own kind.

My wings gave out with Giselle's house in sight, and I tried to aim for the right garden as I plummeted to the ground.

Blackness hit me like a hammer to the head.

"Does she normally shift while she's asleep?" Giselle's voice cut through the darkness.

I groaned and stretched, feeling the rough scales on my hands brush against bare floorboards. My eyes felt as if they were hung with lead weights, but I cranked them open enough to see my clawed feet... and human body. Ah. That's what she meant. *At least I didn't kiss Astor this time.*

Of course, that might be because he wasn't here.

I twitched my feet, which turned back into human ones. So did my hands and arms. "What did I miss?"

"A hell of a concussion," said Will.

"You broke my fence," added Giselle. "I'd charge you if I cared enough, or if I had any neighbours to complain about the mess. Which I don't."

"One piece of good news." I tried to sit up. My head gave a throb of protest, and I sank onto the mattress again. Maybe not.

"Are you feeling okay?" asked Becks.

"Nope." I closed my eyes. "Can you please stop staring at me? It's not helping."

Becks cleared her throat. "Yeah. Of course. Will's been busy brewing that potion for Kit. It should be ready soon."

"Oh, good." At least some good had come out of today's misadventures.

After a few minutes, I managed to sit up, gingerly. The others had gone back to their business—Will to the kitchen stove, Becks to Cori's side of the room—but Giselle stood watching me as though I was some fascinating animal.

"What?" I asked.

"You just fell twenty feet out of the air into my garden," said Giselle.

"Want to know how I survived it?" I ran a hand over my

fragile skull. "Shifters are more resilient than regular humans, and dragon hide is made of strong stuff."

"I don't doubt that," said Giselle, "but if you were trying to keep a low profile, you just put a beacon on my house."

Ack. "Sorry. If it helps, I didn't see anyone following us out of the city."

"It doesn't," she said. "But if they knock down my house next, I'm holding you personally responsible."

For some reason, she didn't sound angry. More amused. Strange, but I supposed that after two years in hiding, I imagined she didn't get much in the way of excitement out here.

"Noted," I said to her. "Did the League ever—ever send other shifters to attack people while you were a member? Aside from those wolves?"

"No. I told your friends that already." Her mouth turned down at the corners as if in distaste. "Those beasts—fae or shifter—aren't like any I've heard of."

Not good. "It has to have been the hunters who sent them, but we couldn't stick around and find out where they're hiding now. Unless Astor knows and hasn't told us?"

Giselle shrugged one bony shoulder. "He doesn't," she said. "Not for lack of trying, but it's easy for people to disappear in a city like London."

"I'm aware of that," I said. "The ones who usually need to disappear are supernaturals, remember?"

"And you found nothing in those records you stole from the witch?" Giselle queried.

"No." What did it matter to her? Either she was simply trying to needle me again, or she held a genuine interest beneath her outward disdain. "The record didn't say who Twill bought it from."

"The guy was sloppy as fuck," Will added from the

kitchen. "I bet he took a week to even notice he'd been robbed."

"We don't know for sure that he was," Becks added. "Since, you know, we got chased off with pitchforks when we set foot in the Avenue."

"Arseholes." My head felt a little better, so I climbed to my feet, mostly to get out of range of Giselle's smirking face. "You don't have to laugh at us."

"Your propensity for making enemies is unlike any I've seen," she said, shaking her head. "That makes two pointless trips in a day. Are you going to make it through a third?"

"Not helping." Will gave the potion such a vigorous stir that he nearly knocked over the pan. "Despite Twill's shitty records, he's not the only person the League bought from. Or stole from. If I didn't know better, I'd say they had links with a major supplier."

"They do," said Giselle. "Or they did."

"Really?" I frowned over at Will. "Huh. Might that be a way to track them down?"

"It might," Will said slowly. "There are only three main suppliers of ingredients in London, that I know of. If one is linked to the League, I might be able to figure out which."

"Really?" I hadn't thought of finding the League that way, but it seemed a more likely route than any alternatives.

"Yeah." Will brightened. "One's been mostly defunct since the invasion—they ship their ingredients over from France, but boats keep getting attacked by hydras or some shit. I don't think the League's operating from overseas, so it's got to be one of the other two."

"Are you sure they're selling to the hunters?" Becks asked. "Even if the League's people are using a different name, I'd have thought the suppliers would have questions about someone who keeps ordering supplies in bulk but never selling them to witches."

"I don't think the suppliers track who they sell to." Will left the stove and crossed the room to the mattress where he'd left his rucksack. "The majority of witches have always lived in hiding since long before the League was a threat. Some grow herbs and other ingredients themselves, but the rarer ingredients have to come from outside. I'll run a search and see what I can find."

He pulled out the phone Giselle had given him and began tapping on the screen.

I let my gaze travel around the room, noting the simmering pan on the stove. "Is that almost ready?"

"Yeah, the potion should be done in a few minutes," Will said. "I didn't know how much to brew, since we can only guess how much iron they used on him. A healing spell didn't do anything."

His words brought a renewed surge of anger at the League. I didn't know how many years Kit had been their prisoner, not where they'd snatched him from either, which would make it all but impossible to track down his human family. If they'd survived the invasion at all.

After scrolling on the phone for a bit, Will walked over to the potion simmering on the stove. "I think it's ready."

"I hope it works." My gaze travelled over to Kit. He was awake but staring at the wall, seemingly unaware of his surroundings.

"Hey." With a bottle containing the potion in hand, Will walked up to Kit's mattress. "We have something that can help you."

Kit didn't even look up. *Oh, man.* We'd had enough trouble getting him to eat or drink, and he'd refused to change out of his prison uniform.

"It'll help." Will moved closer. "The potion will stop the iron—"

"No iron!" yelled the faerie.

"Oh, here we go," muttered Becks as the faerie curled up in a ball, moaning. "Don't mention iron, Will."

"No iron!" the faerie repeated.

"I'll hold him down," said Becks.

"No way," said Will. "That'll make him even more terrified of us. Let me talk to him alone."

"What if he uses magic on you?" She spoke in a low voice, but I could tell from Giselle's expression that she was listening in. Her lips compressed, and her hands twitched as if she wanted to grab a weapon.

"I don't think he will," I said. "He knows we're not the enemy."

"Exactly." Will crouched down next to the mattress. "Hey. Don't panic. We're not gonna hurt you. I'm a pacifist."

"Can he even understand English?" asked Becks.

"Of course he can," said Will. "He's half-blood, so he must have lived amongst humans before they took him. Can't say I know where they caught him, though. I don't know anything about the League's operations outside of London..." He trailed off when the faerie flinched at the mention of the League. "Sorry."

Kit sat very still, his bright-green eyes fixed on the potion. A simple way to tell Seelie and Unseelie apart was the colour of both their eyes and their magic, and bright green meant his fae parent had been from the Summer Court. The magic he'd used to protect us against the gargoyles had been seriously strong. I hoped Will would be quick to get out of the line of fire if he used it against us. It was hard to tell how much Kit knew of what was happening at all.

Will held up the potion again. "It'll stop the pain. I'm not going to hurt you."

"I think all of us being here is bothering him," said Becks in a low voice. "Maybe we should step away."

"Good idea." I shuffled back a few steps. "You okay, Will?"

"I can handle it," he said decisively. "Go on, stop crowding him."

As the rest of us moved back to give them some space, the front door slammed.

"Astor," Giselle called out a moment later. "Mind telling me why you're covered in blood?"

9

Everyone looked her way, except Kit. Astor stood in the doorway, his clothes torn and bloody. Had he been anyone else, I'd have been worried, but Astor looked more like he'd come back from a trip to buy groceries than what I assumed had been a fight. Regardless, I was glad he hadn't been here when I'd transformed, considering what happened last time.

"I told you, the car's not being tracked," he said to Giselle. "Nobody's coming after me."

"Can you see through glamour?" asked Giselle, crossing her arms. "No, because you're not a faerie. How can you know there isn't a fae monster hiding in the car?"

"What did you do?" I peered out the door and spied a brand-new shiny black vehicle parked in front. "Oh, you got a replacement."

"And a lecture." A muscle twitched in his jaw.

For some reason, that made me laugh. "The mages lectured you on road safety? Did they ask *why* a gargoyle landed on your roof?"

"No, because I didn't tell them that. I told them I had a

run-in with a pack of fae monsters. Hard to tell the difference when the damage is the same."

"They don't have any idea where you live?" I asked.

"Of course not," he said. "I gave them an old address of mine to stop them digging into my history."

"And you're sure they won't see through it?" I peered at his bloodied clothes. "Were you attacked?"

"I ran into a group of redcaps on the way to the mages' part of the city to make my alibi more convincing." His gaze went to the corner where our unconscious companion lay. "What's going on over there?"

"While you were out, we brewed up a cure for our faerie friend's iron poisoning."

"What, you did?" His voice held a hint of genuine curiosity. A rarity.

"Yes. If we can get him to drink it, he'll lose the side effects of the poison and will come to his senses again." Or so I hoped.

"Good," said Giselle. "Then you can ask him about what he saw in the Stronghold and send him packing."

"Absolutely not," I said. "Unlike some people, I don't only value others by how useful they might be to me."

Astor's mouth flattened. Evidently, he'd taken that to be aimed at him, which it wasn't. I hadn't the energy to argue, so I headed towards Will in case he needed help.

Will lifted his head. He had several scratches on his face—we hadn't been able to explain to Kit that his fingernails needed trimming, either—but our guest lay slumped on his back, and the potion container was empty.

"Did he—?"

"Yeah, he drank it," Will said. "Then he passed out. I hope it means the potion is working."

"Same," said Becks. "I guess we shouldn't push him on

what he saw during his imprisonment, but it would help if *he* knew where the Moonbeam was."

"It wasn't in the Stronghold when he was imprisoned there." The sound of a door closing told me Astor had gone upstairs.

I turned back to Giselle, who scowled at the faerie. "What's wrong with him this time?"

"He's sleeping off the potion," said Will. "I hope it'll help him. Iron poisoning is no joke. From what I heard, long-term exposure to iron saps a faerie's very essence and can even prevent them from accessing their magic. I'm surprised he managed to defend us back at the house, considering how long he was exposed."

"It stops the faeries accessing their magic?" A chill raced over my shoulders. "That's fucked up."

"Does anything the League does surprise you at this point?" Giselle said. "Besides, there are plenty of regular humans who'd be very relieved to have a way to shut down a faerie's magic."

"They already have one. The whole city's covered in iron." Yet that hadn't stopped the Sidhe and their rampaging army. "Giselle, were they capturing faeries *before* the invasion? They were, weren't they?"

"Obviously." She did not elaborate.

"And?" I pressed. "I'm assuming they took Kit long before the Sidhe attacked this realm, but there's got to be a reason he was Malkin's personal project."

"Your guess is as good as mine." Giselle glowered at me. "Do you think I knew the name and identity of every other prisoner the hunters took in? I never saw them capture any faeries. And I've never been in the Stronghold."

"I know." If Kit had still been in the Stronghold at the time of the Moonbeam's theft, he was unlikely to know anything, but there must be a reason he'd caught Malkin's attention. "I was just wondering why Malkin singled him out the same way he did to Cori and me. He gave me this whole ridiculous story about how he needed our powers to fight off the Sidhe, if they came back, but dragon shifters are far rarer than half-faeries are."

"You're asking the wrong person," Giselle said. "I didn't see them capture any half-bloods while I was a member. It makes sense that they would, though. I've heard faeries can heal themselves of any injury, which would be a valuable asset if the hunters learned to replicate it for themselves."

"And you think *he's* the bad guy?" I indicated the sleeping faerie. "Your priorities are seriously screwy."

"He's not as harmless as he looks," said Giselle. "I can guarantee that."

"He used magic to protect us when we were being attacked by gargoyles," said Will. "I'd say that proves he's on our side."

"On our side or not, he's as much as a magnet for trouble as the rest of you," she said. "I don't have any wards, or whatever it is you use in the city to keep the fae out."

"Why not get some?" I asked. "Iron wards aren't that expensive these days."

"I have more than enough iron," she retorted. "I won't be reliant on supernatural trickery to stay safe."

"It's not trickery, it's common sense." Sensing a losing battle, I dropped the subject. "Will, did you find the details of the supplier the hunters might have used?"

"I'll get back to that." He left the faerie sleeping and scooped up Giselle's phone again. "Honestly, if that shifter hadn't drawn the human authorities, I might have tried using a tracking spell around the mercenary unit to see if the hunters set foot there recently."

"They must have, if they're the ones who set the bait."

Goosebumps prickled up my arms. "And used the Moonbeam."

Nothing else accounted for the beast's absolute lack of reason, and it chilled me to think that one of us might be stripped of our will so easily.

"They must have known we'd come," Becks added. "Question is, are they also the ones who set the fire at the Avenue, or was that the gargoyles? Assuming they aren't working together."

"I'd say that was their work, too," I said. "It makes no sense for them to get involved with gargoyle street gangs when their ultimate goal is to exterminate all of us."

"They're willing to use all the advantages they can get," Will said. "I mean, look how they played Twill against us."

"True," I allowed. "They might've framed us for that shifter's death without the gargoyles being any the wiser."

"Exactly," said Will. "Whether they're in on it or not, the Fanged will sell almost anyone out, given the chance. They're loyal to everyone in their own clan, but humans are an inconvenience and other supernaturals aren't worth noticing unless they're encroaching on the Fanged's territory. Really, they and the hunters are cut from the same cloth… hey, he's awake."

He swooped over to Kit, who'd lifted his head, blinking around in confusion.

Then, without warning, the half-faerie jumped at Will and wrapped his hands around his neck.

10

Will yelped and grabbed the faerie's wrists, trying to pull him off. Becks and I hurried over to help, but neither of us wanted to freak him out even more.

"Hey!" said Will. "Whoa there. Calm down. Can you understand me?"

Kit stopped struggling and leapt back from Will with startling speed. I'd had little experience with half-faeries, but I knew they shared a shifter's speed and agility but paired with a thousand times more grace and balance. The faerie glided to his feet, tugging at the prison clothes he still wore, as he'd resisted all our attempts to persuade him to change into anything else. "Who are you?"

"Oh, good, you're awake," said Becks. "I'm Becks. That's Will, and that's Ember."

"We're shifters," said Will. "Well, I'm half of one. It's a long story. Do you remember anything about the last few weeks?"

The faerie shook his head and sank back onto the mattress, burying his face in his hands. "Not much. Everything is fogged."

"And you're half-blood?"

He lowered his hands. "Yes. Where am I?"

"London," Will said. "Is that where you're from?"

"No. I… I was born in Cardiff." Now he was no longer screaming, the faerie's accent didn't sound local. If he'd been captured before the invasion, it was no wonder he'd reacted so badly to his newfound freedom. The outside world would be completely unrecognisable to him. Hunched on his mattress, he looked around the room, trembling all over.

"You're safe here," said Will. "You can borrow some of my clothes, and we have food and water, too. You're welcome to stay with us as long as you like."

Over on the sofa, Giselle made a sceptical noise. Sensing the need for an intervention, I motioned to Becks to watch the others and strode up to her myself.

"Don't," I said warningly.

Giselle eyed me. "I didn't say anything."

"You didn't need to." I spoke in a low voice. "I don't care if you think faeries are the spawn of Satan: we're not throwing him out on the streets. He didn't even live here in London before he was captured."

"Neither did I, sweetheart. I lived in Essex, originally."

"That's not the point I'm making. Considering what the League put him through, it's a wonder he remembers his name."

"You do realise it's lucky there aren't any more ex-hunters in the house?" said Giselle. "The others might not be so inclined to ignore your extra-terrestrial friend over there."

"He's half-faerie, not from Mars," I said. "And you were their prisoner, too. If ever a situation called for empathy—"

"Don't tell me how to react to trespassers in my own house."

"Trespassers?" I scoffed. "Good lord, maybe I should have given Astor more credit."

"Someone say my name?" said a voice from the hallway.

I managed to refrain from startling. Just. "I thought you went out again."

"As though I'd miss this latest spat." His eyes glittered with amusement. "So your half-fae friend woke up."

"Yes, he did." I jerked my chin at Giselle. "She's decided to act like he's going to draw the entire Unseelie Court to the doorstep. As if we brought him here by choice."

"Whatever you say." Giselle rolled her eyes. "For someone who's the last conscious member of her species, you're doing a remarkable job of trying to get yourself killed."

"Trying? I didn't frame myself for starting fires in central London."

"Starting fires?" Astor echoed. "What did you do this time?"

"Nothing whatsoever."

"Except damage my fence," Giselle put in. "Speaking of which, I'm going to check if it's salvageable."

She left the room, while I briefly filled him in on our ill-fated trip to central London. By the time I was done, the faerie had returned to his position on the mattress and was fast asleep.

"He's exhausted," said Will. "I'd give the potion twenty-four hours before we can see its full effects. What does His Excellency have to say for himself?"

"Nothing," Astor said. "Except that Giselle's at the limit of her patience."

"So am I," I said. "I'm getting sick of always being the bad guy."

"Tell me about it," said Becks. "I'm losing track of all the crimes we're meant to have committed."

"Arson, murder…" Will ticked them off on his fingers. "And making a public scene, of course. Hey, assassin, do the mages think we're responsible for every crime in London as well?"

"No." Astor had taken in my account of that day's events with his usual level of blank assessment. "They do know about the shifters' deaths because two of them found the first gargoyle's body, but that doesn't mean they have any interest in investigating."

"No, that would require them to leave their pretty houses and start slumming it with the rest of us renegades." Will gave an eye-roll. "Forget the mages. It's the hunters who are placing a target on our heads for every other supernatural in London to throw knives at. If Malkin is still mad at us for blowing up his prison, why not come and take his revenge in person?"

"That's what I'd like to know." I swivelled to Astor. He'd spent more time around Malkin than any of us had, and the pair had maintained a cordial relationship right up until the moment Astor had pulled a gun on him. Admittedly, Malkin had called him by a number, not by his name, but Astor was the only person in the room who'd had recent contact with the hunters' leader as a supposed ally rather than an enemy. In other words, the only one of us who could even come close to guessing his current strategy.

"What?" said Astor.

"You know what." Will must have guessed my line of thinking. "Did Malkin ever drop any hints about where he might have relocated to?"

"No," Astor said. "I did hear from several eyewitnesses that his estate was evacuated by helicopter, so he might have flown to the other side of the country for all we know."

"Helicopter?" I snorted. "Of course he had one of those on standby. I doubt he went too far from the city. I royally fucked up his plans and destroyed his prison. I don't see him letting that slide."

"He won't," said Astor. "But the mages don't seem to have a clue about his intention to remove their status at the top of the hierarchy. They're oblivious to anything outside of their own ranks."

"Why don't you enlighten them?" Will said. "I know they don't give a shit if the rest of us live or die, but you'd think they'd want to know the hunters have a weapon that can control any shifter who crosses their path."

"If I told them that without any proof, I'd be out of a job even if they didn't realise my prior connection with the League," Astor said evenly. "We're operating on pure conjecture that the hunters stole the Moonbeam back at all."

"It'd make our lives easier if they hadn't." Hearing Will put their plans in such blunt terms made me all the more certain that our worst fears had been realised. "But no. I bet they used it on the shifters at the Stronghold as well as the one that attacked us."

"The Moonbeam wasn't inside the prison at the time, was it?" Becks looked questioningly at Astor. "If Malkin stole it back, I'm guessing he didn't want to leave it too far from his sight after the last time someone swiped it from his clutches."

"Don't ask me," he retorted. "He doesn't confide the details of his strategies even to his top advisors, and I was skating on thin ice with him because I kept disappearing out of contact. From what I gathered, most of the guards inside the jail also knew the bare minimum. They were as surprised by the order to evacuate as anyone else."

"They just went along with it?" I didn't need to ask why. The hunters had been indoctrinated into believing Malkin's word was law, even to the point when he'd trapped them inside an underground fortress flooded with poisonous gas.

"Of course they went along with it," said Astor with a hint of impatience. "You should know by now that most hunters would gladly die for the cause."

"It's a wonder there are any left," I remarked. "Or maybe there aren't, and that's why he's using shifters instead."

"The shifter who attacked you?" Astor's gaze slid questioningly to me. "Do you really think it was a shifter and not a fae?"

"It was a shifter." My skin prickled as I thought of the open rage in its eyes, the total lack of recognition. "If nothing else, faeries' blood is a different colour to ours."

"You killed it." His voice was neutral, free of judgement, but my stomach dropped all the same.

"It would have killed one of us otherwise." The words rang hollow. While shifters were known for hitting first and asking questions later, that beast hadn't been in control of its own will. "It didn't seem capable of understand that we were fellow shifters, and it also used some kind of magic I'd never seen before against the others. Will and Becks completely froze."

"And Will *dropped* me," Becks added.

"Yeah, sorry about that," said Will. "I've never felt anything like it. Except… well, when Ember shifted."

"What?" I frowned at him. "I've never frozen anyone."

"No, but it's the closest I've seen to what that shifter did," Becks said. "When you first shifted, it was like this wave of terror washed over me and I could barely move."

My mouth parted. "What?"

Astor's gaze passed over my face without meeting my eyes. "Clearly, Ember wasn't affected because she belongs to the same class of shifter as the beast you saw."

I what? I shrank inwardly, trying to banish the memory of how I'd shredded the shifter's throat with my claws. "I don't know what it was, but it sure as hell wasn't a dragon. If the hunters have been breeding hybrids…"

That kind of sick experimentation was in line with the

depravity I'd seen in the Stronghold. Who was to say what other crimes they'd committed since leaving their hideout?

Becks's mouth twisted. "That's beyond horrific."

"Tell me about it." Will looked as if he might throw up. "I'm starting to think that I'd rather take on the Fanged after all."

"Assuming the hunters don't decide to use the Moonbeam on them, too," I added. "We need to find their hiding place. Starting with their ingredient suppliers. Right, Will?"

"Their what?" Astor said.

"The League might still be buying up witch ingredients even in exile," I explained. "Will said there only three suppliers in the country."

"I saw a lot of things in the Stronghold which would be tricky for a non-witch to get hold of," Will added. "I doubt they carried all their supplies with them when they evacuated."

"So?" Astor didn't look impressed. "It's not hard to home-grow plants."

"It's bloody difficult to find a unicorn tail or a living mandrake," said Will. "Both of which they had in their lab.. And they can't be home-growing anything while they're on the run. They'll

almost certainly still be making those bullets at the very least."

"You don't have proof that the bullets were created by supernatural means," said Astor. "They existed long before the invasion."

"No manmade weapon can instantly kill shifters and not humans," I said. "It's not like we're susceptible to iron like faeries are."

"Exactly," said Will. "Face it, Astor, pretty much every-thing the League does ties back to the same supernaturals

Malkin claims to want to eradicate. He couldn't have worked out our weaknesses without tearing us apart to figure them out first. He even uses magic to enhance his own soldiers as well as himself."

"The hypocrite," Becks said. "He doesn't see that he's turning himself into exactly what he fears the most."

"No, he doesn't." Astor paced to the room's corner without meeting my eyes. Evidently, the subject of what Malkin had referred to as enhancements was still a sore point with him. "Malkin has convinced himself that no matter what he does, he's absolutely human, and not a supernatural at all. He's so absorbed in his self-righteous quest that any word against him only registers as white noise."

"I worked out that much when I tried to reason with him," I said. "I thought I knew real evil before, but he…"

"Stop talking about him," Will said suddenly. "You're scaring Kit half to death."

Oh, shit. I hadn't realised the half-faerie had woken at the noise, and had huddled in a ball with his knees against his chest.

"Sorry," I said. He remained hunched up, hands over his pointed ears.

"Kit." Will hastened over to him. "Hey, Kit. Don't panic. It's just us."

Kit looked at him, then at the rest of us. His eyes lingered on Astor. "You… were in the jail. I remember."

Oh, boy. I hadn't thought about how he might react to Astor now he was properly awake. Nor Giselle either. The giant pile of iron weapons didn't help either.

"He's an ally," said Will. "Same as Ember. They both helped you escape."

"That's right." I stepped awkwardly in front of the weapons stash and gave an encouraging smile.

"I remember her. And…" He turned to the neighbouring mattress, where Cori lay sleeping. "Her sister."

"Cori." Just saying her name made my chest tighten. "I'm glad you're okay. We were worried about you."

The tightening sensation gripped me harder as his gaze lingered on Cori. "They put her to sleep."

"Yeah." I'd assumed he didn't want to talk about his captivity, and I didn't want to distress him any further, but I couldn't help wondering if he'd seen the potion they'd used on her. I'd ask a few more questions later, when he'd had the chance to settle in. "We're going to help her, like we did you."

Kit nodded. "Thank you for saving me. I am in your debt."

Uh. If I knew one thing about faeries, it was that they took vows and promises very seriously. Sometimes to the point of death. I wasn't sure if the same applied to half-bloods, and this guy seemed entirely non-threatening, but I didn't need to find myself entangled in some kind of complicated contract with the Seelie Court. "It's all right. I did what anyone would have done."

"Where are we now?" He looked past my shoulder at Astor. "I *do* remember seeing him. With the League."

"He was pretending to work with them to help us rescue my sister." I wasn't sure if that was the right thing to tell him, but it was the easiest way to explain an overly complicated situation. "He's, ah, a taxi driver."

Astor himself looked mildly startled, even though he was the one who'd chosen that unlikely profession in the first place. "That's right," he said. "I was undercover."

The faerie blinked at him. "You don't look like a taxi driver. You look more like you're the lead singer in a failed rock band."

Will howled with laughter, Becks snickered, while I tried and failed to hide my smirk. Astor himself wore an expression as blank as the wallpaper.

Then he said, "Did you hear anything about the Moonbeam while you were imprisoned in the Stronghold?"

Dammit, Astor. I'd planned to keep all references to his imprisonment to a minimum for the time being. Even a miraculous life-rejuvenating potion couldn't undo years of psychological trauma overnight. Kit gave a visible shudder, and I stepped closer to Astor, hissing, "Drop it."

"I didn't see the moon. I haven't seen it in years." Kit gave me a curious look. "Can I see it now?"

"It's not dark outside yet," I said. "But sure, why not."

"Great." The faerie flashed us all a bright smile. "I missed the moon. The sun, too."

Faeries. I'd forgotten what literal thinkers they tended to be. At least he seemed to have shaken off his distress, but he'd get eaten alive if we let him go back into the city unsupervised. What on earth were we supposed to do with him?

"I don't suppose…?" Will began. "You said you were born in Cardiff. Do you know how long it's been since you were last at home? Do you remember the invasion?"

"Invasion?" Confusion clouded his expression. "What invasion?"

"When the faeries came," Becks clarified.

He flinched. "Yes. I remember. They left me in the iron cage so long I nearly starved to death."

"I'm sorry." A lump grew in my throat. "The invasion was two years ago. That's why it's not safe to go outside."

"The dark fae came." Kit nodded gravely. "I'd been in the Stronghold for a few months when they arrived."

"So you were there for about two and a half years?" asked Will.

"I suppose I was." He rocked back on his heels. "You said we're near London. Can you help me get home?"

"It's not easy to get around these days," Will said carefully.

"The public transport services aren't as reliable as they were. Plus, we're kind of on the run, as you might have noticed."

"Ah." The faerie looked more thoughtful than disappointed. "We're fugitives?"

"Yep," said Will. "Sorry about that. We don't even have cool T-shirts."

"I don't have a T-shirt." Kit frowned. "Why am I still wearing these awful clothes?"

"Do you want some of mine?" Will moved over to his rucksack and threw a pair of jeans at Kit. "Come on, leave the others to their shouting matches."

As Kit took the clothes to the bathroom to change, Giselle walked back into the room. "Has your extra-terrestrial friend left?"

"No, and he's half human, which is more human than I am."

"Damn right. So don't even think about attacking him." Becks bared her teeth at Giselle. "He's pretty mellow when he's not panicking. As you can see."

"You'd be jumpy if you'd been stuck in a prison for over two years," I added.

"I was a tool of the League for over half my life," said Giselle. "I understand perfectly well. But I'm not equipped with dangerous magic powerful enough to level a city."

"Faerie half-bloods aren't *that* strong," I said. "He's no more a danger than we are."

"That's hardly an encouraging comparison," said Giselle. "You're all a threat to my secrecy. Do you know how many ex-hunters depend on this shelter? Not only did you fly here with monsters on your tail, you crashed into the garden in full view of everyone around. And now you're expecting me to take care of every inter-dimensional troublemaker you happen to run into."

"Inter-dimensional troublemakers sounds like the name

of a band," said Will. "Hey, if Astor already looks like an ex-rock star anyway, maybe that can be our new career path."

Kit reappeared as quickly as he'd vanished and glided over to the mattress, somehow making the simple movement look as elegant as a ballet dance. Now that he wore Will's jeans and shirt, he looked more human than fae, apart from the slightly pointed ears and his eerily handsome features. He clearly hadn't shaved in a while, but half-faeries had little facial hair, and since they stopped visibly ageing when they hit their twenties despite living normal human lifespans, his age was hard to guess.

Will blinked a couple of times as if becoming aware that he was staring. "Hey, it looks like we have at least one background dancer. Now all we need is the rest of the band."

Kit looked up. "What do you mean?"

"He's joking," I told him. "Don't listen to anything Will says."

"Now we're all here," said Becks. "I'm starving. Do we have anything to eat that isn't tasteless cereal bars?"

"I can run to the supermarket," I offered, "but I'm guessing our host will object to me showing my face in public."

"Oh, for pity's sake," said Giselle. "I'll call for takeout. One of you will have to go and pick it up. I don't give out this address."

The thought of finally getting a decent meal put me in a better mood. Within the hour, we gathered in the living room with cartons of Chinese takeout. Even Astor didn't skulk off, though he kept his distance from the rest of us while Kit spent the last half-hour breathlessly asking us about everything that had happened in the last two years. He seemed to have decided that Astor and Giselle weren't an immediate threat, at least.

"Are mobile phones still a thing?" he asked. "I never liked them."

"You were in a prison, not a time machine," said Astor.

"Cool it," I said out of the corner of my mouth. "You're being rude."

Kit gave him a curious look. "Are time machines real now?"

"Nope," said Becks. "Would be nice to have a do-over, given the state the world's in, but no such luck."

"I don't think it's that bad," said Kit. "You still have movies, right? Can we watch one?"

"We do, but there's no TV here." Will glanced over at Giselle, who occupied her usual spot on the sofa and was studiously ignoring the rest of us.

"It's not my job to entertain you," she said, stabbing her chopsticks into the carton with unnecessary force.

At least she and Astor refrained from scaring Kit too badly. She left the room when we were finished eating, and when Kit had fallen asleep—abruptly, mid-sentence—we returned to the subject of our next move.

"We need the witch supplier's address before we return to London." Will picked up his phone from where he'd put it down when Kit had distracted us. "One's based up in Scotland, but the second operates from inside the city itself. Their supplies are stored in warehouses near the Thames before being distributed throughout London."

"And I'm betting it's the same place those gargoyles showed up dead," I murmured. "Might be coincidental, but I'd say it's worth checking out."

"Under shadow spells," Will added. "We ought to assume everyone we run into in London is on the hunters' side. Or at the very least, not on *our* side."

"Funny how that always happens," said Becks. "I'm in,

provided I don't have to fly again. No offence, Will, Ember, but it's not for me."

"There's no other way unless we take the car." I lowered my voice, conscious of Astor's presence in the room. "Also, Kit definitely shouldn't come with us."

The trouble was, there was an increasing chance Giselle might kick him out of the house when we took our eyes off him, and we no longer had the excuse of him being too fragile to survive on his own.

All eyes turned to Astor, who looked stonily back. "I don't make the rules here. You're lucky she even let you stay."

"We destroyed the Stronghold," said Becks. "Surely rescuing a harmless half-faerie doesn't erase that."

"She feels threatened," said Astor, "because every faerie both of us has ever met has tried to kill us."

"Or been a prisoner," I said. "Is that right? Don't try to justify your prejudice. It won't work."

"I'm more concerned that he'll attack her, because he recognises her as a hunter," said Astor.

I had to admit that was a possibility. "It's okay now he's awake. Besides, I've tried to kill you more times than he has."

A razor-sharp smile flickered across his face. "Right you are, little dragon."

"Don't push your luck," I warned. "You know we can't bring Kit along with us, but Giselle won't listen to anyone except you."

"You have some nerve lecturing *me* about only thinking people are worth paying attention to when they're useful to me."

My mouth dropped open. "Excuse me? It's your idea we're here in the first place. Also, I wasn't talking about you. Stop being so damn touchy."

Astor's mouth thinned. "Regardless, you need to find

another shelter before you're left with no choice in the matter."

"Some chance of that without any money," Becks said. "If every mercenary unit is requesting information we don't have, we might as well go back to the Avenue and take our chances with the neighbours who think we set fires for fun."

"You must have got by before the invasion," said Astor.

"I worked in a bar," I informed him. "Which got trampled by fae. Now we're out as supernaturals, a lot of places rejected us on principle long before the mercs started clamouring for everyone to present ID. And to top it off, half the people on Magic Avenue think we're arsonists, murderers, or both. As for Kit, he's miles from home without any way of knowing if his family's alive or dead."

"I'm aware," Astor said, "but you can't insist on keeping every wayward supernatural you happen to stumble across."

"You can't pretend to be surprised," I said. "You hate my 'overactive conscience'. That's why I piss you off so much."

"Why is everyone shouting?" Kit said sleepily. "Oh, is there a fight happening? I want to watch."

Astor's eyes narrowed. "Sort out your issues between yourselves. I'm not here to police your supernatural problems."

And with that, he left the room, closing the door softly behind him.

"Ray of sunshine, isn't he?" said Becks.

"Did you say sunshine?" Kit peered out the window. "It's cloudy."

"It's a figure of speech," I said. "Never mind Astor. Will, do you need my help making more shadow spells for tomorrow?"

"Yes, but don't change the subject," Will said. "What on earth is going on with you two?"

"Hell if I know." I walked over to the rucksack containing

our supplies. "Giselle's just as bad. She's supposed to be running a safe house."

"Yeah, but you did kind of destroy the garden," said Becks. "I mean, there's a dragon-sized dent in the lawn. It's kinda impressive."

"You just had to remind me."

Between Astor and Giselle, it was safe to say that our days in the ex-hunters' hideout were numbered. Which meant everything hinged on what we found at the witches' warehouses tomorrow.

11

Another restless night had me tossing and turning on the mattress, my mind roiling with images of the day's events. The shifter I'd killed appeared behind my eyes every time I closed them. Around midnight, I gave in and went for a walk outside to clear my head.

As I inhaled the cool night air, my dragon side awakened, yearning to leap into flight. While it would be less risky under cover of darkness, Becks hadn't been kidding when she'd said I'd left a dragon-sized dent in the garden and the fences on either side had been flattened when I'd crashed. I might have avoided the incident if I'd had more practise before I'd attempted such a long flight, but that was entirely the problem. I'd only ever shifted while backed into a corner, and as my encounter with the beast at the mercenary guild had made clear, my dragon side and human side were still at odds more than otherwise.

The shifter I'd killed was a stark example of what happened when that balance was entirely tilted in favour of the beast. Any human left inside the shifter had been subsumed by the animal within. Malkin wanted to do the same to me, given the chance.

I couldn't let him. And it bothered me to know I was still in the habit of thinking of my dragon side as a separate entity whose actions were in no way under my control. When I'd been caught in that violent frenzy earlier, my claws had sheathed in the shifter's body as if they belonged to someone else. The same had occurred when Malkin had commanded me to kill the other dragon shifter back in the jail. I'd been desperate, terrified, and with good reason. But I knew on a soul-deep level that I'd only been able to unlock the full extent of my abilities when I'd let the dragon and human exist side by side without trying to hold back.

Spending more time in my dragon form was the obvious solution, and if I grew more comfortable in that skin, my human side might not be shoved to the background whenever I let my dragon side roam free. It was worth a shot. If I'd had more control, I might have been able to hold back before I took the shifter's life.

Or maybe his death had been a mercy.

I pushed the thought aside and lifted my hands, trying to shift them into claws, but thinking of the beast's death brought a rush of guilt that entirely swamped my shifter side. Remorse was no effective trigger.

I tried anger instead. Focused on my hatred of the Orion League, my soul-deep fury at the people who'd ruined our lives. Heat rushed to my fingertips, and my claws emerged at once, needing no encouragement. I held them up in front of me, marvelling at how the scales blended in with my skin. *Now for the rest of me.*

"Nice gloves, darling."

I jumped and would have sliced Astor's face if he hadn't dodged smoothly in a motion worthy of a faerie. Not for the first time, I wondered how I'd ever thought he was an ordinary human. He'd crept up on me like a ghost.

"Go away."

"That's not friendly," he said. "I came to see where you'd gone."

"That's funny, I thought you were doing your best to avoid getting me alone." I knew I was being childish, but so was he. "I truly don't have space in my life for any more drama, so if you don't mind…" I trailed off pointedly.

He didn't move. "I wasn't avoiding you, but you need to stop provoking Giselle. That goes for your friends, too."

"She wants us gone," I informed him. "I could be a model guest and it wouldn't make a difference. We'll figure a way out of here tomorrow. I'd prefer not to spend any more time indebted to someone who can't stand the sight of me."

"Who, me?" He tilted his head questioningly. "That's what you think, is it?"

"How else am I supposed to explain this?" I gestured vaguely at the house. "Look, I thought we sorted our shit out. You renounced the hunters, saved our lives, and then I saved you in turn. There are no debts between us, so there's no need to act as if I showed up on your doorstep begging for help rather than you manhandling us into your car and driving us to someone who wants us around even less than you do."

His mouth parted. At a guess, he'd never thought of the situation like that. "I didn't see a lot of options. And I'll gladly take you back into the city if you want, but I think that's as likely to get you killed as not."

"Isn't that what you say about all our plans?" I said. "I already told you all the reasons we can't walk away. As she is now, Cori is still effectively their prisoner. That won't stand. I won't let it."

"The Moonbeam won't be at the warehouses," he said. "I guarantee it."

"I'm not expecting to find it there," I said, "but it's the only way to even begin tracking the League without walking willingly into their clutches. And this time you can't pretend to be on their side until the last moment."

"No." He said no more, and though I tried to catch his eye, his gaze was fixed somewhere in the distance.

"And?" Maybe it was too much to expect him to open up to me. "What's the problem?"

No answer came. I turned back to the house and heard a single word, spoken quietly. "Wait."

"For what?" I turned on my heel to find him finally looking at me, the moonlight casting his pale features half in shadow.

"I didn't know," he said. "About the other dragon shifter."

Pain locked around my heart. I tried not to think about him too often if I could help it. The well of grief and guilt was too deep to let myself drown in that sorrow when Cori still needed me.

"I know you didn't." I blinked tears from my eyes. "That was all Malkin. Whatever he did to you isn't your fault either."

"I'm responsible for my own choices," he said. "You don't know the extent of it."

"I can guess." I let my gaze skim over his tattooed sleeves, over the tally marks visible on his exposed collarbones. "You killed shifters. Well, as of today, so did I."

"That's not the same."

"You were *twelve* when you signed up."

"And sixteen when I made my first kill." His eyes were flat, as empty as a starless sky. "I was on my last chance to prove myself after fleeing my first two proper missions. The shifter was a werewolf who'd killed three people, and he nearly gutted me, too."

"You ran away?" I couldn't picture Astor attempting to flee from an enemy. Then again, I couldn't really picture him as a teenager either. "If you think that'll make me have less sympathy and not more, you're wrong."

"That's not what I was doing." His hands fisted at his sides; even his knuckles were marked with faint scars. "What I did during my time in the League—you can barely imagine."

"I bet I can." I clamped my mouth shut, giving myself a mental shake. I didn't need to act like a dick when he'd finally begun to have an actual conversation with me. "I told you before that I believe in second chances. Except for Malkin. He's too far gone to deserve anything but the noose."

He dipped his head in agreement, but his expression remained bleak. "I'm not going to argue with you, but we can't ever be on the same page in this."

A sinking sensation filled my chest. I lowered my gaze. "All I want to know is whether you saw the Moonbeam yourself. After Giselle stole it, I mean."

"Briefly," he said, "but I didn't know what it was at the time. She came out of Malkin's torture chamber holding a bag of stolen artefacts, and I was more interested in keeping her alive than the details of everything she'd taken."

"That was after we met in London." She'd escaped imprisonment during the invasion, so it must have been. He'd been that close to the Moonbeam and hadn't even known.

"Yes." He studied the collapsed fence. "Impressive work. Were you trying for a repeat performance?"

"Without the crash-landing." I glanced back at the house, hoping Giselle hadn't stirred. "Every time I've turned into a dragon has been under duress because someone's been trying to kill me. That's not how it's supposed to work."

"Isn't it?" he said. "You want to practise? I'll tell Giselle you're stretching your wings, if she wakes up."

"Like she'll go for that." Strangely enough, the idea of turning into a dragon with him watching me made my shifter side feel even less like cooperating. "Never mind."

"Forget her." He watched me expectantly. "What can I do to speed up the process? Want me to push you off the roof?"

"I hope that was a joke." He clearly had no intention of leaving, and as flustered as I was, not so much as a hint of dragonfire stirred inside me. "You staring at me isn't helping."

"That never stopped you before."

"The situation lacks urgency." And he hadn't been looking at me as if I was both amusing and deeply fascinating at the same time. "Were you hoping I'd give you a lesson in how to be a dragon shifter? Part one, pretend to be human. Part two—"

"Dye your hair? I like your natural colour better."

His opinion shouldn't matter, and yet heat flooded my face with no sign of a shift to be seen. "So do I, but you know, needs must."

"And you shift later in life than others. You aren't susceptible to the full moon's effects either."

"No." I didn't quite know how to feel about the fact that he'd figured all that out, without me telling him. "Probably because we'd find it even harder to hide if we spent several nights of the month roaming around torching half the countryside."

"Or eating farmers' sheep, like you said."

"Ha." I sat down on a stump that had once been part of the fence. "Seriously, I'm at a major disadvantage if I run into Malkin again and don't strike him dead before he uses the Moonbeam to shut down my human side. I need to gain total control over my dragon form before that ever becomes a possibility."

I regretted being honest almost at once, but his expression turned thoughtful, not judgemental. "Would being in a fight break out your combat instincts? I can help."

"If you want me to snap your neck." Out of the question. My claws could wrap around his throat and twist his head off like a bottle cap.

"You won't," he said confidently. "Also, I'm pretty sure your dragon form isn't *that* strong."

"Don't be too sure." He was deluding himself if he thought he stood a chance against me when I'd hulked out. Or dragoned out, as it were.

"Go on, then." A smile played at the edge of his lips.

Okay, bring it on.

I aimed a punch at him. He caught the blow with such speed that my feet skidded in the grass and twisted my arm behind my back. *Holy shit, he's fast.*

I kicked at him, but he held me at just the right angle to keep my foot from making contact. Shifting would break his grip in an instant, but it was all too easy for my claws to deliver a fatal blow without even trying. Hunters were trained in lethal efficiency, to hit hard and fast with the purpose of dealing as much damage as quickly as possible. In other words, they could kill a regular human in ten seconds. But shifter strength and resilience won out, and I'd easily overpowered the hunters I'd faced once I'd disarmed them. There'd been no need to hold back.

Now? Astor didn't seem to care for the danger, but my shoulder was starting to go numb, and all my attempts to free myself ended in failure.

"This isn't good enough," I growled, half to myself.

"Then shift." His breath was warm on my cheek. "I can handle it."

"Like hell." I twisted my arm, and scales rippled up my wrist before I'd quite realised it was turning into a claw. I tugged myself free with a wrench that caught Astor full in the face. He flew a good five feet into the air, landing on his back in the splintered pile of wood I'd crushed in my dragon form.

"Shit." I trod towards him. He wasn't moving. "Er. Astor?"

Astor got to his feet, blood streaking his face, and gave me a tight smile. "See?"

"If you wanted me to bitch-slap you, you could have just asked me."

"You're more than half-shifted. Look." He brushed bits of wood from his clothes and pointed at my chest. I looked down and saw that not only had both my arms shifted, but scales coated my shoulders and upper chest, too. With my feet encased in clawed feet, I looked like I was cosplaying Godzilla. Minus the tail.

"Are you trying to get yourself decapitated?"

He kept moving closer, until my claws were inches from his neck. My shoulder twinged where he'd twisted my arm, but my sensitive human muscles and bones were now encased in thick scales.

"No. I don't think you'll hurt me."

My claw lifted, the edge brushing against his neck. "That's a hell of a gamble."

"I thought you liked living on the edge, little dragon."

"Why do you call me that?"

He shrugged. "I don't know. It annoys you."

"Yes, it does." My claw nicked the skin of his neck. A thin bead of blood appeared. "Dammit."

"Don't apologise for what you are," he said. "That seems a good place to start."

As if you'd know. I swallowed the bitter words, knowing they weren't deserved. "I'd be less inclined to apologise if things didn't tend to go horribly wrong whenever I shift. The first time, I passed out cold and freaked the hell out of my little sister. The second time, I caused half of Magic Avenue to blame me for every fire-related crime for the foreseeable future. And the third, I wound up on the front page of the local newspapers. We haven't even got to the part where I broke Giselle's fence."

"Some would take that as a badge of honour." He reached down and picked up a sizeable chunk of broken fence. "Would you feel like this is a more even match if I was armed?"

"No!" I raised my clawed hands. "I don't want to kill you, but you're playing with fire, literally. If I fully shift, I might step on you, if not outright attack you."

"Or kiss me again."

"Or—" I spluttered, my face heating like a furnace. "No. Never."

He smirked. "Never. That sounded so convincing."

"You don't want to kiss a dragon. That's the opposite of the sort of thing that happens in fairy stories."

"I wasn't aware we were in one." He swung the piece of fence experimentally. "You're almost there. You might as well finish the job."

Anger rolled around inside me. Was he really arrogant enough to think himself untouchable? After I'd carried his broken, bleeding body out of the Stronghold?

Astor swung the broken fence. I reached out to catch it, and his other fist shot out, fast as lightning, and punched me in the nose.

My eyes rolled back in my skull, my head throbbing with the reminder that I'd suffered entirely too many head-to-floor collisions in the past day. Warm blood dripped down my face.

"You *bastard.*" The word ended in a growl more animal

than human, and my body arched as a pressure built behind my shoulder blades and my wings extended from my back.

It was like being able to breathe again. My wings pumped, my tail flicked against the overgrown lawn, and I inhaled the cool night air with lungs strong enough to breathe in the very flames that flowed through me like blood in my veins.

Astor released the broken fence piece and stepped towards me, wearing a satisfied smile. "See? Now you can turn back into a human."

I don't think so. The wind rushed over me and brought with it a current of fierce joy. My wings carried me off the ground until I flew on a level with the rooftops.

"Ember." Astor waved angrily at me. "Get down. Now. Giselle will murder you."

"She's welcome to try." The words came out in a rumbling growl.

"Ember." I could hear him swearing under his breath. "I'm not kidding, get down *now*."

"You get down, puny mortal." No actual words came from my mouth, but Astor got the gist. Rather than surrender, he approached the house and began climbing up the drainpipe. I stared, perplexed, my wings rising and falling in time with my heartbeat.

"You'd better not wake Giselle." Astor climbed onto the upper windowsill. "Don't you dare fly away."

My wings continued to beat, but I remained still, watching him as he pulled himself up over the gutter and onto the roof. He straightened upright, bathed in soft moonlight, and looked me in the eyes.

"Come on," he said. "I know you don't want to stay in that form forever. You can't talk to people. You can't touch anything without knocking it over."

I can't touch you. I can't kiss you, like I want to. Like I...

Oh, boy. I'd thought those desires had been under lock

and key, but my shifter side was pure instinct, with none of the reservations my human side possessed. She remembered every second of our kiss, of our bodies pressed against one another in the heated aftermath of the shift.

I knew the danger of letting myself want a human. Yet I still wanted to touch him.

Scales receded, wings vanishing, claws becoming hands. My feet stumbled as I landed on the roof, unbalanced with no wings to catch me. As he caught my wrist, I regained my footing and stumbled against him.

My human side returned in the form of a voice whispering, *Good, you shifted back. Now let go of him.*

Astor didn't move. Possibly, he thought I'd fall again if he let go of me.

"That was dangerous," I breathed. "What possessed you to punch a dragon in the face?"

"I sensed you were close to shifting, and that seemed the quickest way to finish the job."

"Sensed?" I echoed. "That's not a human thing."

"I don't have another word for it," he said. "There was a… a charge in the air, like electricity."

A non-shifter shouldn't have been able to sense it, but he was far more than a regular human. "You should let go of me."

"Yeah," he said. "You should walk away."

"Maybe." I didn't budge.

His lips hovered above mine. "I should walk away, too. What is it about you?"

"I'm hot?"

He surprised me by laughing. "Yes, you are, little dragon."

"I'm not little, either. I can shift again and demonstrate."

"I know that, Ember." He spoke my name in a purr that ignited a different kind of fire inside my chest.

Pressed against him, I breathed him in, felt the inches

between our lips electrify as he closed the slight distance between us. I kissed him back, a quiet growl building in my throat as I took control, and he let me, seemed to like it, even. My teeth grazed his bottom lip, my lungs hardly needing to draw breath as I devoured him.

His hands pressed against my shoulders, firmly, breaking the kiss off. His breath came out as unevenly as my own.

"Don't shift," he murmured. "I prefer you like this."

"No danger of that happening."

"You aren't going to breathe fire on me?"

"I could. I can't say I've been this intimate with a human before. You're too breakable."

"Is that a challenge?" He had me pinned a moment later, arms against my sides.

I let him think he'd won for a moment before I flipped him over onto his back. My hand skimmed over the muscles of his upper arms, lingering on the swirling tattoo mark surrounding a mass of scar tissue from one of the many bullets that the hunters had shot him with.

I felt his breath catch as I traced the outline of the symbol, wondering if it had any meaning. "Does it hurt?"

"No," he breathed against my mouth, but there was a new tension in his body that hadn't been there before. I'd been right in thinking he didn't want to engage with the notion of being linked, however tenuously, to something that wasn't human.

Something like me.

A shadow fell over the roof. We both looked up, saw the winged black mass blotting out the moon.

That's no fae.

Instinct seized me, and I shoved him, propelling both of us over the edge of the roof. As we fell, my feet shifted into claws a heartbeat before he landed on top of me and sent us both crashing into a bush.

Astor rolled onto his back and exhaled slowly. "Whatever that was, it better not have seen us."

"Yeah." I groaned. "At least we didn't knock the fence over this time."

"What are you two doing?" Kit stood in the shadow of the house, unseen by either of us. Upon catching sight of us in the bush, the half-faerie flushed bright red and backed away. "I'm sorry for disturbing you."

"Don't worry about it." I pushed to my feet, my face flaming as much as Kit's. "What are you doing out here? Giselle didn't kick you out, did she?"

"No, I came to look at the moon."

"Of course you did." I picked a leaf out of my hair. "Giselle is going to kill us."

"Yes, she is," said Giselle.

12

"What," Giselle said, "were you two doing up on the roof, exactly?"

"Stargazing." Not my most convincing lie, but easier to believe than the truth. "I couldn't sleep and didn't want to wake the others."

"So you thought you'd climb into the most conspicuous place possible when you knew you were being hunted from the sky?"

"The gargoyles never come out here." The beast I'd seen had been no gargoyle, though, I was sure.

"That we know of." She stomped back into the house.

I couldn't even look at Astor. "I'm going back to bed."

Or to cool off. Maybe I should take a cold shower, but I'd have to face the others eventually, and it sounded like Kit was telling them exactly what he'd found when he'd come into the garden.

When I entered the living room, Will snickered loudly. "I thought something weird was going on with you two. You freaked out Kit."

"I'm not freaked out," said the faerie indignantly. "You looked like you were trying to kill one another."

"We weren't. I was practising shifting."

"In a bush?" Giselle raised an eyebrow. "What's with you two? I realise you're a dragon, but you run hot and cold more than any other person I've met. I thought you two weren't even speaking to one another."

I didn't know what was worse: everyone dissecting my relationship with Astor or having to admit that we'd seen what might have been one of Malkin's monsters flying over the house. "This is hardly your business."

"It's my house you keep vandalising," she retorted. "So, yes, it is."

"You two are confusing the crap out of me, too," Becks added. "Just so you know."

"I didn't think there was anything confusing about the way you two were touching each other," said Kit blandly.

Will cracked up laughing. "I knew it," he said. "When I walked in on you two the other morning, I swore there was some weird dynamic going on."

"Weird is right," I said. "Guys, seriously. It's not *funny*, Will."

"Yes, it is," he said. "It's hilarious."

I groaned, sank my head into my hands. "I've never made fun of any of your boyfriends."

"Wait, he's your boyfriend now?"

"No!"

Giselle sighed. "Whatever it is, make your mind up and don't lead him along."

"I'm not leading him along." If anything, it was the other way around. "I gave him the chance to walk out of my life before, and he didn't take it. I don't know what kind of nonsense the League tolerated, but—"

"The League was not what I would call supportive of any

kind of fraternisation, even among our own ranks," Giselle interjected. "I had a taste of that myself, when another a human and I got too close. I found him dead in the harbour the next morning."

My mouth dropped open. "The League did that?"

Will raised an eyebrow. "Damn. Sorry."

"Don't feel sorry for me," said Giselle. "I'm fairly sure most of the people who drop by here think Astor and I are involved, but we aren't. But I swear if I have to watch you two dancing around each other much longer, I'm going to flip a lid. Just get whatever the hell it is out of your system. And not on my fucking roof."

My face flamed. "Look, it's as much on him as it is on me. If he's known that would be the consequence of pursuing anyone for years, it's no wonder. Especially a supernatural."

"Never." Giselle shook her head. "The first thing we learned when we set foot in their training centre was that supernaturals were less than animals."

"I get it," I said sharply. "You know this is complicated. All right? I'm going to sleep."

I lay down on the mattress until she got the hint and shuffled back to her room. Once she was gone, I told the others in an undertone about the winged shadow I'd seen from the roof and the suspicions both Astor and I had about its origins.

"That close?" Will sobered up fast. "Damn. Either they followed us yesterday after all, or they have search parties combing the entire area, not just the centre of London."

"I know." My disquiet had only heightened, and though the others eventually settled back down, my mind remained wide awake.

I went through my rucksack and took out the notebook, turning the well-worn pages in the hopes that the familiar text would bring me back some semblance of calm. Instead, I found myself stuck on the untranslatable section of text again. When I'd run my hand over Astor's tattoos, the thought had crossed my mind that the swirling symbols were along similar lines, but up close, the resemblance wasn't quite exact. Whatever was inked on Astor was more akin to magical runes, or wards… and thinking of him did nothing to calm me down whatsoever. I tossed the book aside and lay back on the mattress, staring up at the dark ceiling in the hopes that my brain would take the hint. Eventually, exhaustion overtook me, and dreams of flight carried me away.

I woke up to Giselle's rasping voice. "No, you can't throw out my weapons."

"I'm not throwing them out, I'm just saying that I'd prefer it if you didn't leave them lying on the floor," Will was saying. "Especially as they're made of iron, and one of us is a faerie."

Here we go.

As Giselle broke into a counterargument, I grabbed some clothes and went to the bathroom to shower and dress. When I returned to the living room, Giselle sat on the sofa, polishing a knife, while the others had joined ranks against her. Except Kit, who sat alone on the mattress and looked as if he was considering glamouring himself invisible until the others stopped arguing. I didn't blame him a bit.

I waved at him. "Hey, Kit. Did you sleep well?"

As he glided towards me, I spied an iron knife that had fallen out of my rucksack when I'd upended it on the floor the previous night. I reached for it and unintentionally kicked the notebook aside, causing it to slide half-open across the floor.

"What's this?" Kit crouched and picked up the notebook. "Why do you have a book written in the faerie language?"

My mouth parted. "You can read it?"

He peered at the page, his brow furrowing. "Yes, but most

of it is in English. The bit that isn't just says, 'The rest can only be read by a true dragon shifter'."

A true dragon shifter? "Are... are you sure that's what it says?"

"I think so." He peered at the page more closely and reread each line. "It's been a while since I read the language, but that's what it says. Who wrote it?"

"I don't know." Questions cascaded through my mind. "What does it mean by a true dragon shifter? Do we not count?"

"It doesn't say." Kit looked troubled. "Should it?"

"No. Maybe." I tried to pull myself together. "That notebook was given to Cori and me by the other dragon shifters, but we were never able to read the part not written in English. We always thought the text was a kind of code, or else a language only known by dragon shifters."

"The other dragon shifters gave you this?" He turned the notebook over in his hands and then passed it back to me. "Then it's precious to you. I won't read it."

"I really don't mind." I didn't, either. Kit was no threat. Giselle was seriously grasping at straws if she thought him as dangerous as the dark fae that raided houses in the night and devoured humans in dark alleyways. "Ah. I saw a piece of paper in your—in your room. In the Stronghold. Written in the same language."

His shoulders hunched as if he wanted to draw into himself. "Yes. He... Malkin... asked me to read it. He'd stolen some documents from the half-faeries. I pretended I couldn't understand a word."

"You were brave."

There came the thud of a cupboard closing as Giselle stomped around the kitchen making coffee. Leaving Kit alone with her was a disaster waiting to happen, but I had yet to come up with an alternative that didn't involve exposing him to the hunters' wrath.

I returned the notebook to my bag and went to join Will. "Are we still going to the warehouse today? All three of us?"

"I think we'll have to." His mouth turned down at the corners when he set eyes on Kit. "We'll come straight back when we're done."

Kit blanched. "You're leaving?"

"Not permanently," I reassured him. "We're going to check something out in London, and then we'll come back."

"You can't leave me alone with them," said Kit quietly, his gaze flickering towards Giselle. "They want me gone."

"I know, but only one of us can fly without making the front page of the newspapers, and I can't carry three of you at once."

"I'm not useless, you know," Kit said. "I can use magic, too."

"I know," Will said, "but half of London wants us dead, and you've barely recovered from iron poisoning. I'm not risking Malkin getting hold of you again."

"You're going after *him*?" Kit sounded horrified. "Why?"

"I hope we don't run into him, but we're going to some warehouses where the hunters might be getting their supplies," I explained. "There are also a bunch of gargoyles swooping around the area, thinking we murdered two of them, so we're expecting a fight."

The faerie's eyes widened. "But what if they follow you back here?"

With a shiver, I recalled the shadow I'd seen the night before. "We'll try not to let that happen, but we have to go into the city. It's the only way to wake up Cori."

"Your sister." His expression clouded. "He—Malkin—he drugged her."

"Yeah." Since he'd brought up the subject himself, I risked

a question. "Did you ever see a shiny black stone while you were Malkin's captive? It's about the size of my fist."

Kit frowned. "No. I don't think so."

"It's called the Moonbeam," I added. "I doubt Malkin walked around showing it off, but I wondered if you heard the word mentioned at all."

"I don't recall." His shoulders hunched. "I… have trouble remembering my time in there."

"Don't worry about it," I said. "You're safe with us. Just hang tight, and we'll be back within a few hours."

Or so I hoped. From the little I knew of the half-fae, honesty was a trait they valued highly. While the stories claimed the Sidhe were physically unable to lie, that wasn't true of their half-human brethren. Kit, though, seemed open and honest in a way which would be difficult to fake. Even when he'd used his magic out of fear, he'd never done so to manipulate or incite terror. That didn't mean he wasn't capable of serious strength, and who knew, maybe he'd be an equal match for the hunters without iron poisoning sapping his will, but I wouldn't force that on him if I could help it.

After we'd shared a few of our considerably battered cereal bars for breakfast, Will handed some freshly made shadow spells to Becks and me. Kit watched curiously as I slid the thin black band onto my wrist.

"What's that?" he asked.

"Custom-made shadow spell," said Will. "It's how we plan on sneaking around under the hunters' noses."

"Becks, try not to tear holes in my leg this time," I added.

"Do you have any idea how scary it is up there when you're a cat?" she asked. "Every gust of wind makes me think I'm going to fall off."

"It won't be for long," I said. "It's that or ride on *my* back, and I don't think you want to do that either."

A loud scoff from the sofa told me Giselle was still

listening in, though she'd returned to polishing her knife with an expression of intent absorption.

"What?" I swivelled towards her. "If you want to offer one of your charming pieces of advice, it's unnecessary."

"Why would I bother when none of you ever listen to me?" She dragged a torn rag over the blade's edge. "Frankly, I'm surprised any of you have survived this long."

"What would you do in our place?" I queried. "Leave the city, condemning Cori to a slow death? Cut all ties and go into hiding? Fuck that."

She dragged the cloth over the blade again. "Better than wandering in half-cocked and getting yourselves killed."

"Or waiting for Malkin or the gargoyles to show up on the doorstep?" I glanced out the window and saw Astor's car had gone. I'd hoped he'd at least offer some solidarity, though I couldn't say I particularly wanted to interact with him after last night.

Over in the corner, I could see Will whispering to Kit. Hopefully giving him some advice of what to do if Giselle really did turn on him. Keeping my fingers crossed that he wouldn't need it, I led the way outside and waited for the others to shift.

I climbed onto Will's back, and Becks tucked herself inside my jacket to avoid the cold shower that greeted us when we flew amid the clouds. At least the murky sky helped to hide us from anyone below, but Becks dug her claws painfully into my chest whenever rainwater slid inside my jacket. It was a relief when we neared the centre of London and dropped below the cloud cover to locate the warehouse we needed. Will had looked up the address, but few maps accounted for the way the faeries' arrival had changed the shape of the city. Skyscrapers had turned into gargoyle nesting spots. Faerie magic had transformed parks into forests and conjured random patches of greenery in the middle of the patchwork of buildings. The Thames snaked through the middle, and as we flew over the warehouses, I glimpsed a huge tentacle lashing out at the bank. Most humans had learned to stay far away from the water.

Pushing strands of damp hair from my eyes, I reached for the bracelet at my wrist and turned on the shadow spell. Beneath me, Will did likewise, and my head spun with vertigo as my brain struggled to grasp the impression of hovering on an invisible steed as we cleared the distance to the ground.

Will touched down, and I felt Becks, also invisible, slide out of my jacket. The street was empty, slick with rainwater, and smelled distinctly of rot. I hadn't been this close to the river for a while, and I'd forgotten how pungent the stench was.

"I forgot to mention we're near a cleanup unit," Will's voice whispered from nearby. He must have shifted into a human again. "I guess they dump all the supernatural-related supplies in the same area."

Ugh. I'd been hoping to use my sense of smell to keep track of my friends while they were hidden by shadow spells, but the rotting stench put an end to that strategy. I kept my ears open for footsteps instead as we trod between warehouses in search of our target. The witches would doubtless have trip-wired whichever one belonged to them, and as a witch, only Will would be able to pick up on and dismantle those defences. We'd have to tread carefully.

A gust of wind swept the stench of dead bodies in my face again. I gagged, holding my breath.

"That's foul." Will coughed. "Smells like a dead troll."

"Or several," I added.

A rumbling noise warned of a loud engine coming this way. I aimed for the gap between this warehouse and its neighbour as a truck rattled past, carrying with it the foul smell of the dead. *It's the monster pickup. About bloody time.* I wondered if anyone had ever bothered to clear up the pile of dead tentacles we'd left at the drop-off point back up north. It was nice to know at least one person in the city was doing their job, but the racket made it impossible for me to keep tabs on Will and Becks.

As the truck passed by, leaving an eye-watering stench in its wake, I slipped out from the warehouses and looked for my friends. They couldn't have gone far, but the truck's growling engine obliterated our footsteps, and with my sense of smell out of commission, I had to rely on my eyes.

Which was why I didn't see the hunters coming until they were almost on me.

I jumped back into the warehouse's shadow as two masked hunters came running past, dressed in black and impossible to mistake for anything else. Both carried guns, their faces were concealed, and they headed in the same direction as the truck.

Curiosity drove me forward. My heart hammered against my ribs as I speed-walked after the hunters, conscious that my overwhelmed senses had me at a disadvantage. I'd lost track of my friends outright. When the truck disappeared around a corner, I spied another pair of hunters standing next to a large, dark shape slumped on the ground like... well, a dead body. And not a human one.

Shit. I halted, trying to make out the corpse's features. Wings? That was a gargoyle, and as I trod a bit closer, I picked up a few words of the hunters' conversation.

"...too close this time," muttered a female voice.

"What did you expect?" said the man next to her. "They can fly. Of course they noticed."

Noticed what? I watched the pair of them lift the gargoyle's inert body and carry it towards a parked car, throwing it into the back with the expert efficiency I'd come to expect of the hunters and then climbing into the vehicle themselves.

I ducked back into the gap between warehouses and stiffened when something nudged my leg. My gaze picked out the shape of a cat, half-visible. Becks. "Where's Will?"

That wasn't him, was it? No, the gargoyle had looked too big, and Will had been in human form the last I'd seen.

The engine started and the car reversed, then headed in the opposite direction to the truck. I memorised the number plate—for all the good it'd do—then began to follow.

Becks's now-human hand caught my arm. "Wait. Will said he thinks the hunters were here to pick up their order, and that's what's in the truck."

"And the dead body?" If the hunters were driving the truck, they must be heading to the same place as the car was, so we could follow either. "I'll see if I can catch them."

Becks swore, then shifted into cat form and padded behind me as I broke into a jog. The car wove amid the warehouses at a speed that would have been hard to keep up with if not for our shifter speed and stamina. Even the city's debris-laden post-invasion streets didn't seem to slow it down, and it left the warehouses behind and began a zigzagging journey north of the river.

Where are they even going? Was this just a supply run? If so, what on earth did they want with a truck full of dead monsters? I wished one of us could have followed that, too, but it was all I could do to keep up with the car. Soon skyscrapers cut through the clouds above, and low-rise concrete roofs hung at slanted angles where the buildings below had collapsed under the magic unleashed by the faeries' assault on the city. The car pulled into a narrow street, and two hunters got out. Rustling above prompting me to lift my head, seeing the gaps inside the office blocks where the shattered windows used to be, now used as gargoyle nesting spots high above the ground.

We shouldn't be here.

Two hunters hauled the body out of the back of the car and deposited it on the ground at the foot of one of the buildings. Somehow, I doubted they were returning the dead gargoyle to their family out of kindness.

Without fanfare, the hunters got back into the car, pulled out of the side street and drove off. As I began to follow, a cat's yowl turned my blood to ice. A screech followed, becoming a chorus,

as three gargoyles converged on the body of their fallen kin.

One held Becks in a strong grip, her feet dangling from the talons wrapped around her neck.

13

ecks. My shadow spell hid me for now, but if hers had worn off, mine wouldn't last much longer either. She struggled to escape the gargoyle's talon, its sharp claw perilously close to piercing her throat.

Hang on, Becks. I'm coming.

I reached for one of Will's point-and-shoot explosives. I'd have to be careful to avoid hitting Becks, but it was that or expose myself before the shadow spell wore off.

The sound of flight filled the air, and no fewer than seven gargoyles descended in a wave of leathery wings and granite skin. Far too many to deter with a single small explosive, and if Becks managed to free herself and run, they'd catch her in seconds. *Okay, new plan.*

I shrank into the shadows as my hand flickered back into visibility, followed swiftly by the rest of me. Shit. Of all the timing. I watched the gargoyles, noting the intelligence gleaming in their yellow eyes. For all their animalistic features, they were human underneath. The part of them that could be reasoned with must be reachable, but their sharp back-and-forth growling did nothing to reassure me that they'd spare us a shred of lenience even after seeing the hunters drive away from the crime scene with their own eyes.

As I debated whether to strike first or grab Becks and run like hell, the gargoyles began to turn human. One shifted, then another, a ripple passing through their group as if some unspoken signal called them to turn from stone statues into people.

Unfortunately, the scary factor didn't abate even in the absence of wings and claws. They looked a damn sight healthier than most humans these days, too, ranging from wiry to muscle-bound, and wore clothes that were in surprisingly good condition. I supposed it must be easy to steal anything you wanted when you could fly. The one holding Becks was a brute, at least six and a half feet tall and wider than two of me put together. Twin knives were sheathed at his belt.

Baring his teeth, he gave her a violent shake. "Talk."

Becks screeched, a high-pitched sound worthy of a gargoyle, and shifted back into human form. The sudden impact of her weight broke the gargoyle's grip, and she landed on her feet, sprinting for her life.

She didn't make it a metre before a wall of gargoyle blocked her path. The hulking man stepped to the forefront. For some inexplicable reason, he was bare-chested despite the bleak weather. Deep scars marked his pale skin in a manner that disturbingly resembled wounds inflicted by a gargoyle's claws. Will had told me the Fanged fought one another in human and gargoyle form for entertainment, and this dude seemed a few cards short of a full pack to say the least.

Cracking his knuckles, he gave Becks a menacing look. "Well? What've you got to say for yourself, little kitty cat?"

Becks glared at him. Blood streaked her neck where his

claws had cut through her fur. "I'm not here to start a fight. We didn't kill your friend."

I held my breath, readied to intervene. Becks was usually more of the hit-first-and-ask-questions-later type, but the odds were so far tilted against her that her best hope was to run.

Then one of the gargoyles—a woman, easily as heavily muscled as her male companions—finally spotted me. "Another one!"

Oh boy. I carefully stepped forwards, holding up my hands to show I was unarmed. "I didn't hurt anyone either."

"What are you doing right next to the crime scene, then?" demanded the big guy.

"Following the hunters." I pointed in the direction where I'd seen their car drive away. "They killed your friend by the warehouses and brought the body here for you to find."

"Liar," hissed one of the others, and a chorus of growls echoed the accusation.

"It wasn't us," I said loudly, holding my hands palm-out. "See? No blood. We didn't touch the guy."

The bare-chested gargoyle grunted at me. "Get over here."

I walked to Becks's side, and the gargoyles closed in until they'd formed a circle around us. Up close, each had a visible tattoo on their upper arm in the shape of a curved claw or tooth. Not a hunter-style tattoo, but one marking their membership of the Fanged.

One man, far smaller than the rest, stepped to the head of the group. "You're still on our territory. That deserves punishment." He spoke in a quiet nasally voice and lifted a knife, a chilling smile tilting his mouth. "What do you all think?"

"I agree." A second, larger hunter stepped forward, his own knife gleaming. "We'll take a little trophy from each of you. A finger, maybe."

"Too generous," another broke in. "We should take one of their hands."

"I've got a better idea. Why not let us go?" I suggested weakly. Will was the one who cracked jokes in these situations, not me. "We were tracking the hunters. If you let us go, we can still catch up to them."

"How? Cats can't fly," said the nasal-voiced man. "And you? What kind of shifter are you?"

The big hulking shifter sniffed the air. "Fuck, it's her. The fire-breather."

Oh, *shit.* Denial would do me no favours, but even my dragon form would have trouble fighting off this many gargoyles at once.

"Is she?" The nasal-voiced guy sounded sceptical. "She doesn't look like much."

"We're wasting time," I said impatiently. "Didn't you see the hunters drive off with your own eyes? If you let us go—"

"It *is* her." Another man stepped forward, his face wrapped in bloody bandages that covered his right eye. The left was bloodshot and swollen around the edges. "That cat shifter? She's the bitch that tried to claw my eyes out."

He must be the gargoyle who'd landed on Astor's car. "You tried to kill us. What did you expect?"

If some of these dudes had been responsible for destroying our house and wrecking Astor's car, then I had no hope of reasoning with them. Becks growled in warning, but the wound on her neck looked nasty, and she'd be in trouble if she didn't use a healing salve soon.

Nothing would get us out of this mess short of me shifting into a dragon, but I couldn't say I was enthused at the idea of causing another bloodbath when the hunters were getting further away with every second we spent trading blows.

"We're all being set up," I told them. "By the hunters. They're the ones who killed your people. You *saw* them."

"I don't believe you," growled the bandaged man. "You sold us out to the hunters yourselves. You and the other witches."

"We really didn't." If they'd associated us with the likes of Twill—and one of them had certainly been at Magic Avenue when his house had been on fire—they were almost laughably wrong. "The witches sold us out, too. Now the hunters are trying to blame us for it, to keep us fighting amongst ourselves while they plot to exterminate us."

I had no doubt that was the eventual goal, whatever they were doing with a truck full of dead bodies.

"It's true," Becks added. "If anything, we should be asking if *you're* working with the hunters, since you're playing into their hands so willingly."

A flurry of growls answered, and the large gargoyle pointed a meaty finger at us. "Tear them limb from limb."

The gargoyles converged, transforming into beasts once again, and a loud *bang* ripped through the air. Not a gunshot, but the more muffled sound of an explosive spell.

Several gargoyles took flight with loud screeches. I looked for Will, but didn't see him behind the wall of wings and talons. The gargoyles surged to left and right, away from the smoking hole in the road where the spell had landed.

I caught Becks's arm, pulling her after me. I had another explosive in my inner pocket somewhere, but Becks had accidentally knocked my spells askew when she'd been clinging to the inside of my jacket, and I was still fumbling in search of it when two gargoyles landed in front of us.

One lifted a talon, and my claw caught the blow with ease, while Becks produced her own spell and threw it into the second gargoyle's face. The blast sent the beast into flight in a beat of leathery wings, while the first freed himself and went for my throat. My claws blocked the strike and retaliated with a blow that sank deep into his chest. Blood showered the ground as I ripped my claws free in a spray of crimson. The gargoyle let out a strangled yell and turned back into the bare-chested man, sinking to the ground in a bloody heap.

Had I killed him? I couldn't stop and check. With Becks at my side, I ran through a gap between buildings. Getting lost in this warren would not be ideal, but it was that or run out in the open. There were no hiding places when our enemies were airborne.

The gargoyle Becks had hit in the face flew in pursuit, talons outstretched, and grabbed her around the middle. She yelled and kicked out, blood blossoming on her chest.

My own claws pierced the gargoyle's flank, and a fountain of crimson spurted. As I reached for her, Becks transformed into cat form and broke free of the gargoyle's grip. I raked my claws across his face, and he bellowed in rage.

"Last warning." I lifted my claw again in warning, and he took flight, trailing blood behind him.

Heart in my mouth, I dropped to Becks's side. She'd shifted back into a human and was breathing, but a dark stain soaked into her shirt, and Will was the only one of us who carried a healing spell.

I could see a shower of sparks rising above the street we'd left behind, another of Will's diversions, but we were deep in the heart of gargoyle territory with no easy way out. I continued to walk, reasoning that we ought to reach the end of the Fanged's territory eventually and most of their fighters were in our rear view. Becks hobbled alongside me the best she could with her injury. My own claws were slick with blood. If I had killed that guy back there, I could no longer claim innocence, and the Fanged would have true cause to hate me.

When we came to the mouth of the alley, Becks slumped onto her knees.

"I'm okay," she wheezed. "Just catching my breath."

"No, you're not." I crouched behind her. "Shift. I'll carry you."

She turned into a cat, and I scooped her up, running out of the alleyway.

Talons grabbed the back of my jacket, tearing through the material and piercing my shoulder blades. I yelled and kicked, already off the ground and rising fast. Becks screamed and clung to me as we rose five feet into the air, then ten feet. It took all my effort to keep hold of her as we continued to gain height, rising alongside the tower blocks with dizzying speed.

A smaller gargoyle flew in below me and let out a sound like a cross between a cockerel and a pterodactyl. *Will.*

At the sound of his voice, Becks slid free from my hands and landed on the other gargoyle's back. My claws emerged, and I lashed out at the gargoyle holding me, causing him to release one side of my jacket. I twisted in mid-air, the tower blocks tilting around me. From this height, the area gained a new familiarity. I'd been carried over this part of the city by another gargoyle, nearly two years ago, when the hunters had captured one of their children. We'd helped them with the retrieval and had saved all the kids the League had stolen, and as a result, the gargoyles had moved out of Magic Avenue and had returned to their homes. I didn't know if that group was still around, but they might be our only shot at making it out of here alive.

I waved frantically at Will, pointing at the massive, gutted high-rise buildings the other gargoyles had built their lair in. More winged shapes swooped overhead, but from this distance, I couldn't tell if any of them were our former acquaintances. I liked our odds over there better than with the Fanged, though.

Having also spotted them, Will flew that way with Becks clinging to his back. I *hoped* they'd recognise us as allies, but it had been years, and I didn't know if the same gargoyles lived in the tower block or if another gang had taken their place.

Worth a try. I waved, calling out to them. "Hey! This bastard's trying to kill us!"

The motion jerked me sideways and my arm slid free of my jacket, but the distant gargoyles made no effort to rescue me. They circled Will instead, masking him from sight.

My other arm slid out of the sleeve, and I fell. The brief flare of panic became anger as my dragon side took over. Wings sprouted from my shoulders, scales coated my body, and my tail extended, steadying me in mid-air. My fall slowed to a glide and then an upward climb towards the gargoyles who'd surrounded Will and Becks.

Something hit my upper leg, sharp but not deep enough to draw blood. The gargoyle who'd held me tried to fly out of range, my torn jacket still hanging from one claw, but I easily caught up. In a sweep of my claw, the gargoyle flew sideways into the already shattered glass of a towering window.

My wings carried me upward to the gargoyles circling Becks and Will, and I growled a warning. *Let them go.*

The gargoyle I'd thrown through the window rose into flight to join his fellow shifters, and the group circling Will and Becks began screeching at the interlopers. I found myself wishing for a gargoyle-human translator so that I'd know the right moment to flee before we got caught in the middle of a gargoyle turf war.

I beat my wings, trying to get to Will. One of the gargoyles seized Becks from his back.

"Hey!" A growl tore from my throat, drawing all eyes onto me. *Holy shit, that was loud.*

But effective. None of these gargoyles had faced a dragon shifter before, and despite their fierce expressions, a murmur of fear travelled among both the Fanged and the others whose territory they'd encroached on.

I whipped around to our attackers and said, "Leave."

The word came out as another rumbling growl, and they scattered, vanishing amid the gutted office blocks. I turned back to the newcomers, hoping that my body language had made it clear my animosity wasn't directed at them, but they'd already begun their descent over the tower block, one still holding Becks.

Will flew after them, reaching the part of the building in which they'd built their nest. The walls had been knocked out in several places, revealing openings into open offices and boardrooms littered with collapsed desks and tangled wires from old monitors criss-crossing the floor.

The entire space was full of gargoyles. Some in human form, others hulking and clawed. Upon seeing me, they surged towards the edge of the open office with a chorus of shrieks and snarls.

The one carrying Becks dropped her onto the floor. Will turned human again, crouching beside her and pulling a band-shaped spell from his pocket. The gargoyles immediately tried to grab it from him.

"It's just a healing spell!" Will swore when a clawed hand snatched the spell away. "Our friend's bleeding to death."

"Tell the fire-breather to leave and we'll give it back." The gargoyle had turned into a fair-haired woman of around thirty years old, with a ropy scar down one side of her face. Holding the healing spell off the ground in one hand, she fixed me with a stare that mingled anger, righteousness, and no small amount of fear.

"Ah, hell." Will looked at me. "Ember's… she's sort of stuck in that form. She won't hurt you."

"I'm not stuck." The gargoyles all stirred at my growl, so I clenched my teeth instead and jerked my head between the healing spell and Becks, hoping to signal that I wouldn't attack them.

The female gargoyle released the spell without taking her eyes off me. Will activated it, and Becks's breathing evened out. I watched, fighting the instinct to shift into a human when my scales might be my only defence against a whirl-wind of claws. While Will healed Becks, a half-dozen gargoyles had taken flight from upper windows and count-less more filled the office from wall to wall and surrounded my friends.

"Please let us leave," said Will. "We helped you once. We aren't the enemy."

Becks turned human again and pushed to her knees. "Ow."

"Don't move," said Will. "They're debating whether to throw us out the window or not. If you were wondering what the growling means."

"They're welcome to," said Becks. "As long as one of you catches me before I hit the ground."

"They also think Ember's evil and wants to kill them," he added. "I don't think they recognise her in that form."

Becks rose shakily to her feet and addressed the female gargoyle. "Remember when we saved your kids two years back? That was Ember. They took her sister, too."

The thought of Cori speared me in the chest. I didn't want to fight with my own fellow shifters when the hunters were out there, withholding the means of waking her from slumber.

"She's a dragon shifter," said the woman. "Is she the one

who's been provoking the Fanged and starting fires on Magic Avenue?"

"No," said Becks. "That's the Orion League. They're back, and they're killing gargoyles. I have no idea why, but they're more than happy to let us take the blame."

Thanks, Becks. I nodded and did my best to look contrite, though it was anyone's guess as to whether it came through.

"That's not what it looked like from here," growled the blond woman. "It looked to me like your friend was killing the Fanged with her own claws. When anyone angers them, we all suffer for it."

"They blamed her for what the hunters did," said Will. "Haven't you seen them? They just drove through here with a dead shifter and a truck full of body parts."

Yes. The truck. Damn. I needed to be human again to speak, but as soon as I shifted, I might well find myself impaled before I could utter a word.

Screeches rang back and forth between the gargoyles who hadn't turned human, and Will's eyes widened. "We certainly aren't."

"What is it?" Becks looked at Will. "What are they saying?"

"That we're working with the Orion League."

"What?" Her eyes rounded. "What gave them that idea?"

"We really aren't," Will called to them. "Why would we join forces with people who tried to kill us? Who kidnapped us and locked us in jail?"

"Isn't this one of your allies?" growled the woman, and the gargoyles parted on either side of her to let a pair of newcomers enter. They carried a limp body between them.

Astor.

14

Shock and panic hit me, and my knees buckled when I landed on feet that now belonged to a human, not a dragon. While I could at least argue better in this form, that didn't change the fact that we were outnumbered by a mile and that Astor hung limply from his gargoyle captor's claws, seemingly unconscious. How had he ended up here? Had he followed us?

"Let him go," I told them. "He's not a hunter, and neither are we."

The fact that Astor wore a semblance of a hunter's uniform did not help matters, but at least he wasn't carrying a gun. *Dammit, Astor. What were you thinking?*

The female gargoyle looked between us, her eyes narrowing. "Really. What is he, exactly?"

"He's… a friend," I said. "An ally. Whatever you think he did, he's not your enemy."

"He was caught trespassing. Spying on us, no doubt."

As she spoke, the gargoyle holding Astor a violent shake. I winced, though he still didn't stir.

"I doubt he intended to do either of those things." If I

knew Astor, he'd have been following the hunters, just like us. Why else would he have come here? Part of me wanted to shift into a dragon again and scare them into dropping him, but in his current state, one rough shake might be the end of him.

"Trespassing isn't the same as committing murder," Will spoke up. "The hunters did that. They killed at least two gargoyles in the past week, and it's only a matter of time before they target someone from your clan next."

His words kicked off a riot of screeches that did nothing to help my headache. I'd pushed myself hard by shifting twice in a twenty-four-hour span, and I'd need to do so at least once more if I wanted to leave this place in one piece. With Astor.

I tried to approach him, but the gargoyles closed in, driving me backwards until I stood alarmingly close to the sheer drop.

"Hey!" I said to them. "Don't any of you remember me? I helped save your kids, two years ago. We helped each other fight off the hunters."

"What do you think, boss?" called out another gargoyle. "Should we give them a shove?"

The scarred female gargoyle scrutinised me. "We'll bring them down below. If any of them starts shifting, aim to kill."

"Whoa!" I kicked half-heartedly but didn't dare unleash my claws, not even when I was lifted off the ground and bodily carried from the room.

More gargoyles seized the others; Becks hissed in a catlike manner but went limp, and Will gave a couple of objections that the gargoyles swiftly silenced. Astor vanished entirely as they carried us beyond the office door into the corridor beyond.

We crossed to a dark stairway, and we descended at least three levels before emerging into another open office.

Clawed gargoyle hands dug through the pile of junk on the office floor and produced two cages, and my captor threw me into one of them.

I landed flat on my back, legs sprawling. As the door slammed, I lifted my head and nearly knocked myself out cold. Ow. The cage definitely wasn't made for a human.

Grimacing, I rolled onto my front in an attempt to find a more comfortable position. Will crouched in the cage next to me with an equally uncomfortable Becks lying curled up at his feet.

As the gargoyles left the room, Will looked sideways at me. "Ember, this wasn't one of your best ideas."

"My idea?" I lifted my head. "What part of this was remotely my fault?"

"You went after the hunters."

"I thought that was the whole point in us being there." I rubbed my bruised forehead. "I was hardly going to let them run off with a dead body and a truck full of monsters without scrutiny."

"I know, but I nearly got into the witches' warehouse." Will sounded annoyed. "Another minute and I'd have been in able to find out if the hunters are getting their supplies legally under an alias or if they're stealing spell ingredients as well as bits of dead monster."

"I don't think it matters if they're doing it legally."

"No, but we don't have the full picture." Will tried to sit up properly and groaned when he hit his head on the cage's ceiling.

"I can work some of it out." I spoke in a low voice. "The hunters killed that gargoyle because the Fanged know they're up to something near the warehouses."

"And planted the body in the place most likely to cause trouble," said Will. "What I don't get is why the assassin decided to follow us."

"Does he ever tell any of us his plans?" I flexed my hand into a claw, relieved that at least the gargoyles didn't have access to the drugs the League had used to stop me shifting, and grabbed the cage's bars.

Will hissed a warning and gestured to a gargoyle crouched just outside of the office with his back to the wall. Another stood on the door's other side. While they'd brought the three of us downstairs, there was no sign of Astor. Where had the gargoyles taken him?

Becks shook her head at me. "Sure, he just happened to be driving here, miles away from mage territory or wherever else he spends his time. It doesn't have to do with how he's infatuated with you or anything."

My cheeks burned. "If that was true, he would have just told me."

Would he? If we didn't get him out of here alive, I'd never have the chance to find out.

I reached for the bars again, and a sizzling noise prompted me to look more closely at the others' cage. The bars behind Will appeared to be in the slow process of melting.

"They didn't check all my pockets," he muttered in explanation. "I also managed to drop a tripwire spell on my way in, but I didn't see where it landed. Once that dude outside steps on the wrong bit of floor, we're out."

"Right." The gargoyle did not look as if he intended to move anytime soon, though. "And you're sure they won't kill Astor first?"

He might be maddeningly impossible to communicate with, but I was hard pressed to think of a reason for him being here other than wanting to help us.

Screw it. The cage's bars cracked under my claws. Will swore under his breath. "Or instead of being stealthy, we can just break everything."

"Dragons aren't made for stealth."

I climbed out as Will kicked the melted bars of his own cage aside. The gargoyle at the door heard the noise, but he didn't make it one step into the room before a blast took him off his feet and sent him crashing straight through the floorboards.

"Ah," Will said. "So that's where the tripwire landed."

The blast had taken a chunk out of the floor, but it was easy for my shifter speed to clear the jump and land on the other side. Will joined me and helped Becks climb over too. She was a little unsteady on her feet, but Astor had been in worse shape and I hadn't the faintest idea where the gargoyles had taken him. I might have tried to sniff him out, but the gargoyles' scent covered the whole tower, and I was pretty sure the truck of dead monsters had fried my sense of smell.

"Did either of you see where they took Astor?"

"Nope." Will pressed himself flat to the wall as someone passed over the floor above, their feet visible through the gaps in the floorboards overhead. "This place is a death trap on every level."

"Can you hear what the gargoyles upstairs are saying?" I whispered. "I bet they're talking about him."

"It's his own damn fault for going solo," Becks muttered.

"You don't mean that." Astor was on our side, unequivocally. "He got hurt coming after us. It'd be a dick move to leave him here to die in gargoyle territory."

Will gave an exaggerated sigh. "Ember, if we die for his sake, I swear I'll follow you around as a ghost forever and make you regret your life choices."

He slipped away, heading for the stairwell. Becks and I waited at the bottom for a minute, trying to listen in. The gargoyles' shrieking was unintelligible to me and sounded the same tonally whether they were uttering death threats or just talking about the weather.

Within a minute, Will returned. "They've got him upstairs. *Way* up, near the top of the tower."

"They're not planning to push him off?" Alarmed, I climbed onto the lowest stair.

Will caught my arm. "There's easily fifteen of them on the floor above. The safest route is by flight."

"Safest?" Could I take on a hundred gargoyles even in dragon form? Let alone without Astor getting hurt?

"Fly on my back, then."

"That's even less safe." Will could at least blend in, though. "Fine."

"I'll go on foot," Becks offered. "I'm small enough in cat form to escape notice, and I have one explosive left."

"So do I. Better make it count."

Will and I left the staircase and peered through doors until we found an open office that had been turned into another storage room. The broken windows were blocked by a pile of defunct computer monitors, but my claws easily swept them aside and cleared an escape route.

Now for the tricky bit. Will shifted into gargoyle form, and I climbed onto his back, acutely aware of how exposed I was.

Find Astor. I kept that thought at the forefront of my mind as we flew up, towards the chorus of shrieking gargoyles and the thunder of footsteps that grew louder and louder the closer we drew to the top of the tower.

Gargoyles filled every inch of space on the rooftop, and more still hovered above. I clung to Will's back with one hand and spied Astor. They'd locked him in a cage, placed close to the tower's edge, and appeared to be arguing enthusiastically about what to do with him.

Will reached behind his back, and I caught the glint of a

point-and-shoot explosive spell as he took aim and lobbed it amid the bickering gargoyles.

Pandemonium broke out. Some gargoyles took flight immediately, while the ones already in the air scattered in all directions, a few crashing into one another. As we flew amid the melee, a gargoyle swiped at us and missed, instead hitting another shifter, who retaliated by punching their attacker in the mouth.

Nobody could create a brawl more effectively than a bunch of gargoyles. In seconds the air was thick with flying punches. I jumped down from Will's back and ran to Astor's cage, ducking in and out of the fighting until I reached the platform's edge. Astor was awake, to my relief, but his eyes were unfocused and he looked a little groggy. How hard had they hit him?

"Hey. Astor." I grabbed the cage door in my claws and ripped it off, tossing it aside. "I'm gonna get you out of there."

He gave me an incredulous look. "Are you trying to get yourself killed?"

"I might ask you the same—*ow*." A gargoyle punched me in the shoulder, but it was just Will trying to get my attention. Although the fight raged on, some gargoyles had noticed their prisoner making a not-so-subtle getaway and were making a beeline for Astor's cage.

"Now would be a really good time for an escape route, little dragon."

"I'm on it," I said, and shifted into dragon form.

The shift came on so fast that the gargoyles didn't realise what was happening until my wings flared out and knocked several of them over. My claws splayed across the roof in front of Astor's cage, and I ducked my head to indicate for him to climb on. Claws grabbed at his heels as he did so.

I spun around, fixing the gargoyles with my most

menacing stare. Several of them sensibly backed off and gave Astor the chance to climb behind my neck.

I took flight, in a gust of air that further unbalanced the approaching gargoyles. Will stayed below—looking for Becks—and I positioned myself in front of him to swipe at any gargoyles trying to get near us. When I glimpsed a tabby cat sprinting through the melee, I let myself rise higher in flight. She jumped onto Will's back. A gargoyle tried to grab her, but Becks released an explosive spell that kicked off another punching match between our winged adversaries.

When we were clear of the tower, I rose upward in a swoop that made Astor swear loudly in my ear. I climbed in height with strong wingbeats until we were hidden among the clouds.

"You okay, Astor?" The words came out as a growl, but he got the gist.

"Freezing to death," he grumbled, and I felt him shifting up and down my neck as though my scales were uncomfortable. They probably were. I was surprised he'd climbed on without a fuss, but then again, there'd been no other way out.

I had a thousand questions about how he'd managed to get caught in the first place, but they'd have to wait until we landed. For now, I ducked my head and concentrated on flying, and the rhythm of my own wing beats swept the city away.

15

As I flew down over Giselle's back garden, Astor jumped off. The sudden movement unbalanced me, and I misjudged the landing, shifting into a human right before I fell headfirst into a bush. At least it wasn't the fence this time. I lifted my head and saw Astor laughing at me.

Climbing to my feet, I flipped him off. "You're a terrible passenger."

"You try flying on a giant lizard."

"I prefer flying *as* a giant lizard." Though my body really hurt now, after shifting twice in a day and then flying back at such a punishing pace that I'd left the others in the dust. Picking leaves out of my hair, I asked, "Did you leave your car behind?"

"Since you decided to give me a ride, yes." His brief amusement faded. "The mages will be asking questions. It's miles away from their territory."

"Forget the car. Why did you follow us?" That, I didn't get. "If you'd wanted to come along in the first place, we could have coordinated. Then you wouldn't have ended up dangling off a tower block."

His lips compressed. "I didn't know the hunters were going to be there any more than you did."

"Really." I wasn't sure I believed him. The level of secrecy he'd been indulging in recently was downright maddening, and I hadn't a clue what to make of it. Especially after our encounter last night.

"Yes, really." He sounded a little annoyed. "I was tailing their car, actually. I was running errands for the mages and I recognised one of the hunters' vehicles."

"You're still working for the mages?" I asked incredulously. "And you followed the hunters in *their* car?"

"You'd do the same if you knew how much they offered as a starting salary," he said. "Besides, it's useful to have access to their resources."

"Not when you get captured by gargoyles. "

"They crept up on me when I was following the hunters. Like you."

"I can't believe they nearly threw you off the tower."

"You were worried about me, weren't you?" He smirked, and warmth flared inside me. The memory of our tussle in the bushes the previous night arose to the surface, but my concern for the dried blood on his face tempered my dragon side's interest in revisiting that moment.

"I'm worried about you now," I said. "Get a healing spell. You were out cold earlier."

"Ember?" Kit stood in the back doorway, barefoot, wearing one of Will's shirts and a pair of jeans several sizes too big for him. He looked a little wary, as if he'd expected to see us wrestling in the bushes again. "Where's Will? And Becks?"

"Behind me. I flew back fast." I hadn't been conscious of

leaving them behind, but I'd wanted to make sure Astor was okay.

"You flew?"

"Yeah? I'm a dragon. Will told you, right?"

His frown remained. "I haven't seen you shift before. Why so fast? Were you in trouble?"

"We kind of got captured by gargoyles. Don't worry, none of them followed us."

Astor made for the house without offering a contribution. Kit and I followed him through the back door and into the main room.

"The prodigal dragon returns," said Giselle, looking up from the sofa. "What've you done this time?"

"Had to rescue Astor from a horde of angry gargoyles." I rummaged around in my bag for a healing spell and found one lying at the bottom. Healing spells were pretty low-key as far as witchcraft went, but Astor still wore a stony expression as I pressed it into his hand. "It won't turn you into a toad."

Giselle snorted. "If you were one of us, you'd avoid magic, too."

"No, I wouldn't." I might have pointed out that her tattoos were magical in nature, but I wasn't sure Astor had told her. If he hadn't, that wasn't a revelation that would be welcome coming from me, so I held my tongue.

He did use the healing spell, so I felt safe leaving him inside the house while I went out to wait for the others. I watched the sky, breathing a sigh of relief when Will descended at a lopsided angle with Becks clinging to his back.

The moment he landed, he shifted back into a human. Becks slid from his back, shook herself, and then transformed, too. "That was rough."

"Are you both okay?" I asked.

"Your wings' air current almost sent us flying across the English Channel," said Will accusingly. "Otherwise, yeah, we're fine. Where's the assassin we all risked our lives for?"

"In the house. Sorry. I didn't plan on shifting *twice* today."

"You're still on your feet," Will said. "That's an improvement on the last time. I guess your midnight training session with Astor came in handy after all."

"Please don't," I said, as Becks made a revolted noise. "Let's get inside."

Astor had left the room and Giselle had returned to her position on the sofa, while Kit was still seated on his mattress. To my relief, Giselle seemed to have chosen to ignore him rather than continuing to argue for his immediate dismissal from the house.

"Is everyone all right?" Kit looked Will and Becks over anxiously. "Ember mentioned gargoyles."

"And hunters." At that, he flinched, and Giselle fired a sharp look in our direction. 'Unfortunately, the gargoyles captured us before we could find out where the League are hiding out now."

Giselle grunted. "If you ask me, you picked the right group to get captured by. If it were the hunters, you might not have come back."

"There were five hunters at most," I pointed out. "As opposed to a few hundred gargoyles who were also under the mistaken impression that we're the ones killing them off, not the hunters."

Becks sucked in a breath. "I don't get that. I mean, if the hunters want to take out the gargoyles, you'd think they'd use a more direct route than sneakily murdering them one by one, unless they're more cowardly than they pretend."

"Honestly, it sounded to me like they were trying to remove witnesses," Will remarked. "I tried to eavesdrop on them a bit, and I got the impression that the gargoyles are a low priority. The League's more interested in supplies, but I can only guess why they wanted that truck."

"That was really them?" said Becks. "What in the world would the League want with a truck full of dead faeries?"

"Probably nothing good," I muttered, thinking of the strange shifter who'd attacked us yesterday—and the other one I'd seen flying over the house last night.

"Dead *faeries?*"

Oops. I'd forgotten about Kit, and he was listening to our conversation with an expression of open horror.

"Unseelie monsters," I clarified. "You know. The sort that eat humans. There are pickup spots where the local monster-hunting units drop off the bodies. We used to work for one."

"For about two weeks," added Will. "The pay's shit, and half the time the cleanup crew doesn't even do their jobs. It's no wonder the hunters were able to drive off with one of their trucks."

The faerie's gaze sharpened. "Dark fae? The League is stealing the bodies of dead Unseelie?"

"Apparently." Ill at ease, I scanned the room, wishing Astor had come in to offer his own perspective on the events. "They killed a gargoyle near the warehouses, and when we followed them, we lost sight of the truck. I don't know where they took it."

"We never even got into the warehouse," said Will.

"We wouldn't have found anything if they've been stealing supplies rather than acquiring them legally," I reminded him. "The local covens are going to be pissed off if it's true."

"Knowing our luck lately, they'll find a way to blame us instead," said Becks. "And we haven't exactly helped matters by fighting the gargoyles in self-defence."

"Yeah." I didn't know if I'd killed any of the Fanged during our clash, but it would be impossible to claim innocence should we run into them again. "We can go back later. It'll be easy to find that truck again if it's still around, given that stench."

"Assuming they didn't abandon it somewhere," said Becks. "Since, you know, they're probably as aware of the smell as we are."

"You didn't already learn your lesson?" Giselle's sharp eyes picked over us. "I can't begin to understand what kind of a mess you've entangled yourself in with those shifters, but the League isn't going to make it easy for you to find their hideout."

"You'd think they'd want us to find them so they can enact some heinous new torture on us," I said. "Have they forgotten we exist?"

"I'm insulted," said Will. "I thought Malkin had a special interest in Ember, at the very least."

"Oh, he does," Giselle said darkly. "You took him by surprise at the Stronghold, but Malkin isn't known for making the same mistakes twice. He'll have a strategy, and he'll want to take your friends out of the picture before reeling you in."

"That's why I should go with you." Kit spoke up. "I can sense the fae. I can help."

"Everyone within ten miles could smell that truck," Will said. "And I don't want *you* within a mile of them, frankly."

Giselle cleared her throat. "If you're going to be fool enough to go after Malkin again, I'd prefer for all of you to go at the same time. That way you're all out of my hair. I've had it with bloody dragons landing in my garden."

"If I hadn't turned into a dragon, Astor would probably have taken a dive off the top of that tower block." Where had he gone? Upstairs? I went to look, mostly to avoid another argument, and had one foot on the stairs when Astor appeared at the top. "There you are. Giselle was about to kick us out."

"No, she wasn't. If she was, she'd have been louder about it." He descended in his usual light-footed manner and made for the front door. "I'm going to get my car."

"What?" I raised a brow. "The one you left way over on the other side of London? Tell me you're not serious."

"If I don't, I'm out of a job." Having opened the door, Astor slipped outside. "I already ruined one car this week."

"Is it worth getting killed over?" I hurried to catch him up and attempted to block his way, but he sidestepped me again. "Astor! You can't possibly think you can sneak in and out of London without being noticed. Either you'll run into the hunters again, or else the gargoyles will come back to finish the job."

"The mages' car is our best shot at catching up to that truck," he said. "I thought that was your plan."

"You'd know if you actually contributed." I threw up my hands. "I'm beyond sick of you sitting in on our plans for long enough to steal the best bits for yourself and then ending up in trouble because you can't bring yourself to be a team player."

A smirk tugged at his mouth. "You think I'm stealing your ideas?"

"Yes, you insufferable arse." I folded my arms across my chest. "It's not *funny*. My friends risked themselves for your sake, too, you know."

He exhaled in a breath, serious again. "I'll do my best, but if we want to get back into London tomorrow, we'll need transport that isn't bright red and winged."

"Steal a car?" I gestured at the handful of broken-down vehicles left on the street. "There's no shortage of options."

"Yes, there is. They're all either too small or too conspicuous."

As he began to walk away, I swore under my breath and

then followed him. "You know there might be redcaps lurking out here. Or worse."

It wasn't dark yet, but Astor didn't seem to be in a rush. He dismissed every car on the street for increasingly pedantic reasons and was halfway through the neighbouring ones when I heard the distant rush of wings beating over the rooftops.

I scanned the sky and saw a dark, winged shape above the terraced houses. Tensing, I grabbed Astor's arm and pointed. The creature hadn't spotted us yet, but it was plain to see even from a distance that it was no regular shifter. It didn't have the stone-like appearance of a gargoyle and was covered in more fur than feathers.

It had to be the same winged monster from last night.

I kept my eyes trained on the winged shadow as I crossed the road, hoping to draw it away from the house. At the street corner, the beast veered towards us. Letting out a screech half like a gargoyle, half like a crow, it descended in a spiral of wingbeats that brought it onto a level with the rooftops.

"What the hell *is* that?" I lifted my claws, gauging its size. Smaller than my dragon form, but larger than any gargoyle I'd seen.

"No idea." Astor, too, reached for a knife, taking aim.

A bang sounded, and the shifter dropped out of the sky. Giselle stood at the road's end, her mouth flattened in concentration, one of the hunters' guns pointed into the air.

"You're out of the house."

"No shit." She pursed her lips and limped towards the fallen shifter. "Looks like it came alone."

"That's it?" I caught up to her. "Were you following us?"

"I thought that beast would come after you," she said. "It's been circling the house all day."

Astor swore. "You never told us that."

"And *you* never told me you saw anything last night," she retorted. "I expect that level of secrecy from you, Ember, but Astor? Really?"

Astor paced in behind her. "I assumed we were the ones it was sent to find, not you. It never saw us last night."

"You'd better be right." She reached the fallen heap of fur and claws, poking it with a foot. "Dead. At least they aren't immune to bullets."

"What is it, though?" I crouched beside the body, shuddering inwardly. "It's like a shifter, but…"

Wrong, was the accurate word. Or *twisted,* like a hybrid of shifter and fae, stripped of all capacity for reasoning. As if Malkin had used some magical means to create a monster that combined the worst of both worlds.

"If you're going to dissect it to find out, don't bring it into the house." Giselle turned and limped away.

I stared at the beast until my eyes watered. "Malkin did this," I murmured.

Astor didn't reply, but I knew he was thinking the same. Whether Malkin had guessed our hiding place or not, he was tightening the noose, and all we'd achieved that day was cementing our enmity with the gargoyles.

If this did come down to an all-out conflict between us and the hunters, would our fellow supernaturals fight alongside us at all?

16

———

"I think it's safe to say we're fucked," Will said the following morning as we laid out our plan for the sixth or seventh time. While we were all on the same page—Astor included—that didn't mean we agreed with how events were going to play out that day. "If the hunters' base is swarming with monsters *and* Elites, and we don't even know where it is…"

"We don't have to walk straight in there once we figure it out," I said. "We can follow the truck, then come up with a plan of action when we know where it's going."

The others had been understandably shaken by our close call with the winged shifter the previous day. While Will had offered to brew a tracking spell to trace where it had come from, the process would take hours, and there was a depressingly high chance the local dark fae would have devoured the body long before the spell was ready. He'd expressed annoyance at Giselle for shooting it down before we could try questioning it, but none of us were willing to openly challenge our grumpy host after Astor and I had hidden the shifter's former appearance from her.

"Odds are, if we follow the truck, it'll take us straight to them," I said. "I'd say flight is the best way to keep up. The truck didn't go anywhere near gargoyle territory."

"Doesn't mean they won't be watching the sky," said Becks.

"Agreed," said Will. "I think we should drive, then one of us should take to the sky once we've checked if there are gargoyles around."

"You mean *I* should drive." Astor himself was acting as if nothing whatsoever had changed in the past day, but he also wasn't excluding himself from the plan either. Even if he did keep poking holes in it. "What do you suggest we do when they see us?"

He made a good point. "We can park far enough from the gargoyles' territory that it won't be an issue."

"Then we'd have to follow on foot."

"Shadow spells can be used on objects other than people," Will said. "I made a whole batch, so we can cover the whole car if necessary."

"No chance," said Astor. "How the hell am I meant to drive if I can't see the car? Also, I'm pretty sure people will notice four people floating above the ground."

"We'll be under spells, too," said Becks. "You know, it's not a bad idea."

"It's a traffic accident waiting to happen," Astor objected. "Besides, they'll still be able to *hear* us."

"Not with the racket that truck was making," I said. "It's not ideal, but it's better than being gargoyle bait."

"Agreed," said Becks.

"What do you mean, four people?" Kit said. "You're not leaving me behind again."

"You definitely don't want to come along," I said. "If the truck does take us straight to Malkin's lair, we're not going to let you fall into his clutches again." I'd thought he wouldn't be a fan of following a truck laden with dead faeries either, even the monstrous sort.

"I do." He looked at Will. "I know you think I'm weak, but I can defend myself."

"I don't think you're weak," Will said, "but you've just recovered from iron poisoning, and I can guarantee wherever the hunters are hiding will be covered in iron."

"I didn't think you were going inside their lair today anyway." The faerie's jaw set. "And I defended you from enemies once before, remember."

"From the gargoyles," Becks said. "The hunters are a different story."

"I can put a shield around the car," Kit said. "Like I did when the gargoyles attacked. Remember?"

"Glamour," I said, recalling his defence mechanism. "That's right. You can turn invisible."

"Invisible." Astor's tone dripped scepticism. "I don't want you using spells on my car."

"Don't you remember he stopped a house falling on us?" I asked. "If he's willing to volunteer, it's worth a try."

"Fine," said Astor through clenched teeth. "Let's get this over with."

"We appreciate it," Will added to Kit. "Even he does, though he'd rather jump off the gargoyles' tower than admit it."

"It's my pleasure." Kit brightened and followed us outside into the street, where Astor had parked the car. Unprompted, he glided over and rested his hands on the roof. The surface rippled like a pebble hitting a lake, and then the whole car vanished.

"Seriously?" Astor turned on Kit with his hands curled into his fists. "You made my car disappear? How are we supposed to get into London now?"

Kit shrank away from him. "I didn't. It's still there."

"It is." Will reached out a hand and rapped it against the air. A hollow ring told me the car was indeed still present, and when I extended my palm, I felt smooth metal beneath.

"It's glamoured," said Kit. "Only people with the Sight can see it. That means the gargoyles and the hunters won't have a clue we're there."

"Thanks for this," Will said. "You might have just saved our necks."

"How the hell do we get inside, genius?" Astor reached for the spot where the door had been—or rather, where it still was—but was unable to grasp hold of the handle.

"Easily." Kit snapped his fingers and the car appeared again, as if it had never been gone.

"Better than a shadow spell," said Becks, climbing into the back. "Let's go."

"Yes, let's." I cut Astor a warning look as I got in the front. He seemed to be in a prickly mood today, which was understandable given the circumstances, but I didn't need him taking out his anger on Kit. We all needed to be on the same page if we were to stand a chance in hell of finding the hunters' hiding place—and if necessarily, getting in and out of their new lair in one piece. *With the Moonbeam.*

Astor maintained a stubborn silence throughout the journey, but Kit kept up a steady flow of conversation, continuing to question us about everything he'd missed while he'd been a captive of the Orion League. I gathered that Giselle hadn't been an eager conversationalist. He insisted on grilling us about recent movies and seemed disappointed that new entertainment had been in short supply since the faerie invasion.

"At least we still have *Lord of the Rings*," he said, and he proceeded to lecture us on the difference between Elvish and the faeries' language for twenty minutes while Will tried not to laugh and Astor got progressively more and more irritated.

Personally, I welcomed the distraction, and the relief of knowing that Kit had recovered so well in such a short time. He certainly must have powerful magic to be able to cast this level of glamour, and the car remained unseen all the way into the city. When we reached central London, Astor had to drive carefully in order to avoid colliding with other vehicles whose drivers were unable to see us.

As we drew closer to the docks, it became clear that the gargoyles weren't the only adversaries we might have to contend with. Outside the window, I spied a group of figures dressed in black cloaks moving amid the warehouses with a level of quiet efficiency that rivalled the hunters.

Kit stopped talking, while Astor's hands clenched on the wheel. "What are *they* doing here?"

"Mages?" Will craned his neck to see into the wing mirror from behind my seat. "Damn. Maybe they're looking for that car you lost."

"Or they figured out the hunters are stealing from the witches' stores." It had to be the mages. Nobody else wore those long black cloaks. Except the necromancers, and they had even less cause to be here than the mages did.

Astor slowed the car. "I'm not driving any closer. Wasn't one of you going to look out for the truck?"

"I don't hear it." Or smell it. "I bet the hunters have changed their plan now the mages are here. They won't want to draw their attention."

Astor swore and smacked the dashboard with one hand. "So we're just going to sit here and wait?"

The car trembled as a resonant howl sounded, reverberating in the air and vibrating through every cell in my body. Chills iced my shoulder blades.

"What in hell was that?" asked Becks.

"I'm going to classify it as 'not good'," said Will.

"Shit," I said. "I think that was one of those—"

A giant furred beast came bounding into view, trampling through the broken glass and debris outside an abandoned café.

"Shifters," I finished.

In the absence of the hunters, the beast would all but certainly be able to sniff us out under the glamour. It was huge, the size of a large bear, like the shifter which had attacked us before. Sharp teeth slavered as it turned towards our position, catching our scent.

"Astor!"

Swearing, he put the car into reverse, but not fast enough. The beast leapt, its heavy body collided with the car's front in a sickening crunch of metal. I raised my arms to protect my face from the shower of glass as the car swerved and skidded, trying to dislodge its unwanted passenger.

The beast roared, swiping at the broken window. Pinned to the seat, it was all I could do to fend off the beast one-handed while Astor brought the car to a halt. I batted the shifter's paw aside with my claw and tore off my seat belt, knowing that we'd be exposed the instant we left the car. With the glamour in place, the mages would still be able to see the beast seemingly attacking thin air, but once we were out, they'd see our faces. There would be no hiding from them.

The beast roared and clambered onto the car's front, the bonnet crumpling beneath its weight and its claws tearing at the roof. Astor swore explosively, shoving his door open and rolling out of the car as its foot punched through the shattered window and crushed the steering wheel.

"Get out of the car!" I yelled at the others, sinking into my seat as I tried to get the door open. The handle wouldn't give. *Ah, shit.*

I glimpsed Astor with a knife in his hand, and he tackled the beast from the side and sank the blade into its flank. Blood fountained out over the shattered windscreen, and I slid to his side of the car, out of Astor's open door. The wound hadn't been deep, but he must have hit a major artery, given the amount of blood pouring out of the beast's side.

"It's dying." He stood tense, eyes on the car. "Everyone out?"

"Just about." Will helped Kit climb out of the back. "Shit. We need another ride."

The beast's cry faded to a more human sound. The creature's fur receded until a man lay in its place, dressed in ragged clothes, and bleeding heavily from deep wounds.

"Shit," Becks said quietly. "He really is a shifter."

"Shifter." The man's voice was slurred, his eyes bleary when they tried to focus on me. "You're the one they're after."

"The hunters," I murmured. "They did something to you. Right?"

"Changed me." He coughed, pressing a hand to his bleeding side. "They… the moon…"

The Moonbeam. "We need to get it away from Malkin."

"Too late," said Will, pointing over my shoulder.

A half-dozen mages approached, their long coats swirling in the breeze. One lifted a palm, and a bolt of lightning struck the ground in front of me, sending a wave of static through the air that made my hair stand on end.

I tensed, heart thumping, as several more bolts struck at intervals around our group with deadly precision. The message was clear. If we moved, we'd be fried.

"Shit," Becks muttered. "Should we use our spells on them or talk our way out?"

"Neither will work," Will said out of the corner of his mouth. "They're the fucking *mages.* We're doomed."

Six mages fanned out in front of us. I'd never taken on a

single mage in combat, much less a half-dozen of the reported most powerful of all supernaturals. Sure, they looked more human than we did, dressed in their expensive clothes with their polished boots and fancy haircuts, but the predator in me would have seen an equal even if I hadn't been able to detect the charge in the air that engaged all my senses. The buzz of static in my ears. The shimmering outline around each cloaked figure. And the smell, which I could only describe as the scent of power itself.

The man who'd thrown the lightning bolt stood in front, a tall, broad black man whose eyes seemed to shimmer with silvery white light. Every hair on my body stood on end. This, I was sure, was someone who could run circles around the hunters.

A pale, brown-haired woman stood on his right, giving no indication what her ability might be. That was the danger with mages—you didn't know what you were up against until the last possible second—and the reason I didn't want to provoke a fight unless we had no other option.

Even Astor hadn't moved an inch. I waited, breathing quickly, ready to shift into my dragon form at the first sign of an attack.

"Put your weapons down, shifters." The lightning mage's gaze travelled over us, lingering on Kit with open mistrust. "If you use magic, or shift, you die."

17

"Come with us and none of you will be harmed," added the female mage. "We've let you run wild around the city long enough."

"I think there's been a misunderstanding." No shit. Did even the *mages* think we were to blame for the current trouble in the area, whether that included stealing from the witches as well as the gargoyle's deaths? "We were attacked. We defended ourselves."

"You've been connected to more incidents than the one today," said the lightning mage. "At least two murders have been reported in this area, and with the violence we just witnessed from yourself and your friends, I'm sure you understand how this looks."

Dammit. The shifter's blood on my hands was impossible to hide even if the mages hadn't witnessed the end of our clash. "Did he look like a regular shifter to you? He was— changed. By the Orion League. They're weaponizing shifters for their own ends."

"Do you have proof of these claims?" the lightning mage enquired. "We've received a number of complaints in recent weeks mentioning a dragon shifter in the company of a gargoyle and a cat shifter. I assume that's the three of you."

"It's a lie," I said. "We're being set up—"

My mind exploded. Pain ripped through my head and my vision doubled as my hands moved behind my back of their own accord and an invisible force pushed me to my knees.

The mages hadn't even moved. What had they done to me?

"Stop that!" My wavering vision directed me to the female mage, whose faint smirk told me she was the source. "Let go of me."

"I don't think so." Her mouth flattened, her eyes hard. "If you shift, I'll double the pain. I've no interest in hearing petitions from animals like you."

Animals. Even the mages didn't see us as people, even as their fellow supernaturals. Teeth gritted, I forced myself to my feet, even as my knees buckled under another psychic assault. The others stood rigidly in a tight-knit group, Kit hiding at the back, Becks and Will in front, and Astor at my side. I wanted to warn him to hide before they realised who he was. What had he been thinking? Deceiving the mages was like dancing near the jaws of a sleeping dragon. Of course they'd caught him.

"Oh," said the female mage. "That's interesting."

"Yes, Lady Clare?" enquired the lightning mage.

She jerked her thumb at Astor. "This one," she said, "is human. He's also an employee of ours, Lord Smyth."

Understanding flitted across Lightning Dude's face. "That's who left the car out here. I wondered."

Damn, they found Astor's car. Maybe I shouldn't have stopped him from retrieving it the previous day, but Astor's employment status was the least of our problems.

"Is he, now?" asked a pale-skinned mage with a buzz cut

and some serious bulk hidden under his long cloak. "Under who?"

"Lord Crawford, apparently." Her brow furrowed, as if she was concentrating hard, and she didn't take her eyes off Astor. "He appears to have given a false background when he applied, enough to fool our initial checks."

Was she reading his mind? I'd never met a mage with that ability. It was supposed to be one of the rarest, if not an outright myth.

Even Lightning Dude—Lord Smyth—looked a little startled. "How did he slip past our radar?"

"He's no shifter." Lady Clare's eyes were glass chips. "He's an *Elite*. A member of the Orion League. Lord Smyth, he should be killed. Immediately."

The steel in her voice brought a chill to the air. Lord Smyth himself didn't move for a long moment. Then came a rush of static that prompted me to extend a hand to push Astor out of the way of a bolt of lightning aimed at where he'd been standing.

A white flash dazzled my eyes, red spots dotting my vision. Astor fell to his knees beside me, his nose bleeding, his eyes squeezed shut.

"Stop," I said to the mages. "He's not with the hunters. He's an ally. Besides, we need to go. We're hunting *them*—and we're running out of time."

"I take it you're the dragon shifter?" asked Lord Smyth. "I'd advise you not to make the situation even worse for yourself than it already is. You're wanted by the human police for questioning in connection to a number of crimes, but any punishment they impose is nothing to the consequences you'll face should you attempt to resist arrest from the Mage Lords."

Astor pushed to his knees, bleeding from the nose, and glared at the mages. "I am *not* an Elite."

"Stop hurting him." I moved in front, earning another bolt of pain to my skull. "Would you just *listen* to us? You're supposed to have a policy of fair and balanced judgement."

"You're in no position to be making demands," said Lady Clare. "You and your fellow shifters might get lucky if you should surrender your Elite ally. I've no doubt that if we dig into his history, we can find proof of countless more violations of the law."

Lord Smyth nodded. "The League are too big a threat to allow an Elite to walk free."

They are? I'd known the mages were on the League's list of eventual targets, but I'd thought they were entirely oblivious to the scale of the danger they presented. The regular human courts were positively lenient compared to the leaders of the supernatural community. The Mage Lords were judge, jury and executioner when it came to supernatural crime, and what transgression was worse than belonging to the Orion League?

But Astor's not with the League. And the Mage Lords didn't have a clue what they'd done by cornering us. They didn't, I was sure, know whereabouts the League was currently hiding. Neither did we, but I was willing to bet they hadn't figured out the hunters were raiding the witches' stores and the monster clean-up to boot. If they had, they'd have come here sooner.

The trouble was, we had no guarantees whatsoever that the hunters would actually show up, and it would be just our luck if they'd decided to take the day off. Granted, they wouldn't have sent that shifter here if they weren't in the area, surely.

I faced Lord Smyth, searched his face for any trace of compassion. "He's not an Elite. He helped us bring down the Orion Stronghold two weeks ago. If you're going to insist on breaking into his mind, you'll be able to find that out for yourselves."

"Quiet," Astor hissed out of the corner of his mouth. He doubtless hated having his privacy violated regardless of what information Lady Clare unearthed, but I refused to let them execute him. That was no kind of justice at all.

"We're hunting the Orion League ourselves, and that shifter there was sent by them." I jerked my chin towards the man's crumpled body. "They used some kind of magic to change him, to take away his will."

"No item in the League's possession can do any such thing," Lady Clare said. "Now, surrender your friend or die alongside him."

"They have the Moonbeam." I laid down my last card and threw a plea at the universe in general that the mages knew what I was talking about. "That's what they're using on those shifters. Maybe the gargoyles, too."

"What?" Lord Smyth lowered his hands to give me an incredulous look. "The Moonbeam? That's a myth."

"It's real, and while we're here bickering, the enemy's using it against us," Becks said with barely concealed impatience. I glanced at her, worried, and saw Kit and Will exchanging whispers. Hopefully, they were making an escape plan.

"Give us a chance," I told the mages. "If the hunters are in the area, we can find them ourselves. If you won't allow that, at least give us a fair trial. Including Astor."

"I don't think so." Lady Clare stepped forward.

A loud rumble rose in the background, hidden behind the hum of static conjured up by the mages' presence. *The truck.* The hunters *were* here, and if they came upon the mages... well, even the hunters might avoid an outright fight.

The trouble was, of course, a truck that resembled one

used by the cleanup unit would not register to the mages as a threat unless the hunters actually got out of the vehicle.

"They're here." I pointed over the nearby warehouses. "They stole a truck. That's how they're getting around."

And stealing fae monsters' corpses, but I decided not to add that part. My claim had caused enough incredulity already.

Two of the mages outright laughed, while Lord Smyth raised his palm again. "That's enough. Take down the Elite and bring the others in."

The other mages closed ranks. Lord Smyth lifted a palm, and the broad-shouldered mage behind him conjured up two handfuls of fire, taking aim at Astor.

The air tore apart in a flash of lightning. Astor jumped out of the way, right into the path of the second mage. As flames filled the air, scales shot down my arms and legs, cloaking my body as my clawed feet hit the road and wings sprouted from my back. I positioned myself in front of Astor, and the fire mage's attack simply bounced off me.

Will and Becks both shouted aloud, and I spun around. The remnants of a collapsed building rose in the air as though pulled by an invisible force, forming a wave of shattered brick and glass. One of the mages must have telekinetic powers.

I took to the sky. A tongue of flame leaped from my mouth, over the mages' heads and into the oncoming debris. Every shard of metal and brick was obliterated in one dazzling instant.

There was no hiding now. I'd shown what I really was.

Lightning flashed. I dove, grabbed Astor in my claw and carried him out of the way from the mages' converging attacks. Below, Becks had turned into a cat to dodge the elemental assault while Will was in gargoyle form, Kit already climbing onto his back.

Time to fly. Becks jumped onto Kit's shoulder, and Will flew up to join me, and we soared above the warehouses.

An air current caught us in midair and sent us surging back in the opposite direction. There must be a weather mage amongst the group, too. I flapped my wings frantically, fighting the torrent of whirling air, while bolts of lightning sizzled past, burning holes in the road.

Will vanished, as did the other two. Either Kit had used glamour or someone had put on a shadow spell, but mine was out of reach now I'd shifted into a dragon and was encumbered with Astor in one claw. I beat my wings again, rising higher, as the clouds rumbled and rain sheeted down, drenching me all over and soaking Astor, too. With a roar of frustration, I kept pushing against the wind current, cursing the mages for making it so bloody difficult to get out of here without harming anyone.

The wind eased a little, and a glance downward showed me the mages scattering when a firework went off further down the road. Silently thanking Will, I regained control and flew high over the warehouses. A flash of green light indicated the others' location, right above the large truck. Whether it was the same one as yesterday, I didn't know, but we'd have to fly closer to see if the hunters were at the wheel.

"Ember," Astor hissed from beneath. "The gargoyles."

A winged shadow in the sky warned me that we weren't the only shifters who'd taken to the sky. The Fanged wouldn't stick around if they realised the mages were present, but the rest of us were all too visible. I dropped further in height and landed behind a set of bins one street in front of the truck, putting Astor down before turning human again.

He staggered a little, his hair dripping wet. "That was unpleasant."

"Are you okay?" I asked.

"No thanks to you." He wiped blood from his mouth. "Your claws nearly stabbed me a few times."

"I figured you'd prefer that to being struck by lightning." I kept an eye on the vehicle making its rumbling way between the warehouses. "We need to check it's the hunters driving that truck."

"And how are we supposed to follow it if they are?" he enquired. "Even if your faerie friend hides us, those mages will knock us out of the sky."

Good question. There was no way to follow the truck from the air without getting caught by the gargoyles or the mages' storm. Which left one option. Not a particularly nice one.

"Ember!" Becks raced over to me, Will and Kit behind her. All were considerably windswept, but nobody had any obvious injuries. "Are you okay?"

"Sure." I looked to Kit. "Thanks for the help. Do you think you can glamour us again? Just for a minute."

"Of course," he said, beaming. "I can see why you like flying so much. It's fun."

"If I can point out the obvious," Astor said irritably, "we haven't a hope of keeping up with the truck even if we manage to avoid being exposed."

"No, we haven't." I drew in a breath. "I think our only option is to jump on the truck and hitch a ride."

"We have to ride in the dead body truck?" Becks grimaced. "Ugh."

"At least it'll hide our scent."

"You've got to be kidding," Will said. "Shit, you aren't. Well, it was nice having a sense of smell for a while."

"Absolutely not," said Astor. "I won't put myself at the League's mercy."

"It's that or let the Mage Lords fry you to death," I retaliated. "You'd think there'd be something against that in their employment contract."

Astor glared bloody murder at me. "This is going to get us all killed."

"So is the alternative." I gestured to the sky, where gargoyles dodged bolts of lightning and rising flames. It looked as if the mages had spotted the Fanged intruders, which should at least keep both occupied for a bit.

"Can you put a glamour on us now?" Will asked the faerie. "I'll fly to the front of the truck to see if it's definitely the hunters."

"Absolutely," said Kit, with one of his dazzlingly handsome smiles. There was a burst of green light, and the others disappeared. Including Astor. I heard him swearing under his breath, but his anti-magic attitude would have to take a holiday if we were to survive.

The truck roared around the corner. Beneath, I heard the faint beating of wings, and then Will's voice. "Yeah. It's them."

The vehicle didn't slow, roaring past without any signs that the drivers had recognised us. Or the mages, though the bolts of lightning in the sky would have made their presence obvious. The hunters would want to avoid catching their attention. This was our chance. I crept closer, seeing the back of the truck was padlocked, but my claws would take care of that.

"I'll get the doors," I whispered to the others. "Stick together."

The roar of the truck's engine drowned out their responses, but I hoped they'd heard me.

I made for the truck at a dead sprint, leaping for the back. My claws slid out and easily broke off the padlock, ripping the doors open.

The stench of faerie flesh made me gag. At least most of the space was filled with bin bags, so I wouldn't have to actually touch the bodies, but as soon as the hunters stopped the truck, they'd know someone had broken in. The floor dipped, telling me Will had landed behind me.

"Is it just you?" I whispered.

"Kit's with me, and I think Becks is riding on the roof."

"Hope she's careful. Where's Astor?"

"No clue."

I swore. Maybe he'd run off to do his own thing again, or else silently hidden himself elsewhere. "How long will the glamour last, exactly?"

"I don't know," Kit said. "It depends if he stays within range of me."

So be it. I climbed properly into the truck and positioned myself facing the back so that I could take in the occasional breath of clean air, but the stench of dead faerie was overwhelming and my shifter senses made the whole experience twice as miserable. Kit kept making quiet whimpering noises, and I felt a thousand times worse for him than I did for myself. Even though the faeries in here were beasts that had killed humans, their blue-tinted blood was the same as any fae, and the Unseelie often smelled putrid enough when they were alive. Eyes watering, I tried to breathe as little as possible and spoke little to avoid opening my mouth.

After a few endless minutes, Becks spoke from somewhere above. "We're heading for the river."

"Is that why the smell is getting worse, not better?" Will said in strangled tones. "They aren't making another stop to fetch a dead hydra, are they?"

As the truck began to slow to a crawl, I reached out and pulled the doors closed so that we'd at least have the element of surprise on our side when the hunters checked on their cargo.

When the truck ground to a complete stop, Becks whispered, "I'll go and see where we are."

The door nudged open a little—just enough for a cat to

slip out—and we waited for a tense few seconds before she returned.

"There's a boat," she whispered. "The truck's drivers are talking to some people who came off the boat. Hunters."

"The hunters have a *boat?*" Was that how they were smuggling their supplies to their new hideout? "We have to get on board."

"No thanks," said Will. "They might have decided to try their luck with the local kraken, but I don't like our chances of escaping an enclosed space like that."

"Maybe that's where they're based now," Becks murmured. "Offshore."

"Maybe." Was that why they'd been impossible to find since they'd left the Stronghold? Malkin had escaped via helicopter, which made their potential hiding places almost infinite, but he'd have wanted to keep an open route back into the capital. The sea was more dangerous than the land, or so I'd thought, but then again, any marine monster was no match for the hunters' weapons.

"Let's get out of here." If the hunters weren't going to come for their cargo yet, I wouldn't give them a hand in discovering us.

I opened the doors properly, waited for the others to join me outside, and pushed them shut. It wouldn't do a thing for the broken padlock, of course, but one look at the nearby pier pushed all other thoughts from my mind. Two hunters stood conversing with a larger group, and more still were visible on the open deck of the boat docked at the pier. The vessel wasn't big enough to host the entirety of the hunters' forces, but they might have a few dozen or more people on board for all I knew. The surface of the Thames resembled thick black tar, masking the monsters hiding beneath.

I crept closer, picking up a few words of their discussion.

"The mages?" a burly man was asking the pair who'd

come from the truck. "You didn't pick up our supplies because of the mages?"

"The head of the mage lords himself was present," one of the drivers protested. "With five others. We were outnumbered."

"For your own sakes, I hope you're being honest," said a familiar voice—mild, but laced with threat.

Ice slid down my spine. None other than Malkin himself emerged from the boat, walking leisurely along the platform as he surveyed the docks. "The Mage Lords have had no cause to investigate the warehouses, not if you've been as careful as I advised."

"We have, sir." The driver's voice shook just a little. "They weren't looking for us. The gargoyles—"

"I told you to take care of that little problem, too."

My hands clenched so tight they trembled. *It was all him.* He'd had the shifters murdered to hide his tracks.

"They're persistent," said his companion. "And they're angry. So are the mages. They'd have killed us if we'd stayed."

"Yes, they would have," said Malkin in dispassionate tones. "I did tell you to avoid leaving such a conspicuous trail if you didn't want the Mage Lords to notice our activities in the capital."

Bastard. Malkin had no reason to fear retribution from the Mage Lords if he wasn't even based in the city any longer, but he'd run a major risk by coming here in person.

"Now bring in the cargo." He waved at a set of crates on the bank. "Quickly. It wouldn't do to linger so close to the mages' field of operation."

I held myself still, waiting for the inevitable exclamation from the back of the truck.

"The lock's broken," one of the hunters called out. "Ripped clean off."

"Really." Malkin took a step forward, drawing my attention to how close to the pier's edge he stood. "Is anyone hiding in there?"

No, thank god. I continued to wait, relieved at the foul smell masking my scent, as the hunters began carrying the sacks of dead meat towards the crates. We needed to get on that boat to find the hunters' base, unless Malkin already had the Moonbeam with him. From here, all I could see were the guns stashed in his belt over the same military-style jacket he'd worn the last time I'd set eyes on him. I doubted he'd fought in a real battle in his life, except for the imagined one against my fellow shifters.

It would be so easy to push him into the water. Yet I knew from our last encounter that he wore some kind of spell that created an invisible shield between him and anyone who tried to attack him. The only way we'd managed to temporarily neutralise it had been via one of the League's own magic-suppressant darts, and we had none of those to hand.

As the hunters continued to carry crates of dead monster onto the boat, I trod along the pier. My heartbeat drummed as my dragon instincts registered the unpleasant closeness of the water, but I forced my eyes to stay on my target.

Green light flared across my vision, and Kit appeared in a furious blur of light, his hands at Malkin's throat. An instant later, the half-faerie was sent flying into the air. In the same second, my friends reappeared in a flicker of glamour—Will reaching out towards Kit in horror, Becks frozen in cat form, and Astor on the pier's edge next to the boat.

As Kit landed sprawled on the bank, I grabbed an explosive and threw it down, aiming at the planks directly under Malkin's feet.

The pier gave way, wooden planks folded inward, and water crashed over my head, choking my lungs. I flailed and spat out mouthfuls of filthy sludge as I struggled upward, to see if I'd brought Malkin down with me.

A hand gripped my arm, hauling me out of the water. I gasped and spluttered, my vision obscured by the hair clinging to my face. Someone had a death grip on me, and it sure as hell wasn't one of my friends. As I lifted my head, peering through strands of wet hair, I saw Malkin himself looming over me with fury etched on his features.

Nearby, Astor lay pinned beneath two hunters with his arms twisted behind his back. Another held Becks, in cat form, a gun pressed to her head.

The water's surface rippled, and Will flew out in gargoyle form, clutching Kit in one talon.

Two hunters immediately fired at them. As they swerved and dodged, Malkin hauled me along the platform to the boat. Two hunters grabbed me roughly by the shoulders and threw me—literally—onto the deck. I landed hard on one arm, agony screaming up to my shoulder.

Another more muted jolt of pain drew my eyes to my other arm, and the dart protruding from the skin. *Shit*, I thought, as the world went blank.

18

I woke what felt like several seconds later, lying on a hard surface. My arm throbbed, suggesting I'd broken or sprained it when I'd landed on the deck, and the absence of my shifter resilience made me feel weak, shaky.

They'll break you if they catch you. Astor's words prior to my first attempt to take down the League rang through my sore head. I clenched my teeth and managed to sit up, finding myself in a small cabin containing nothing but a bed and a small sink in the corner. No window, so no way to tell our location. From the lurching movement underfoot, we might well be halfway out to sea, for all I knew.

And I couldn't shift. Not even my claws were within my reach until the effect of the poisoned dart wore off.

Minutes passed, and nobody came into my tiny cabin. Probably for the best, because I quickly discovered that my dragon side's dislike of water also extended to seasickness. After heaving over the sink, my body gave out and I collapsed onto the bed, groaning when we hit a particularly rough wave. The boat itself couldn't be the hunters' main base, so we must be heading somewhere else. Had we guessed right in assuming they were based offshore now? If so, that would mean our destination was the new Orion Stronghold.

At least Cori isn't with us this time. I clung to that silver lining, however flimsy it might be, and tried to forget that our main advantage last time was that Malkin had believed Astor to be on his side until the last moment. That was no longer an option.

Eventually, the door to my cabin clicked open and Malkin entered the room.

"Fuck off," I rasped.

"We'll have to see about that attitude of yours," said Malkin. "You'd be wise not to endanger your friends any more than you already have by bringing them here, Ember."

"I didn't bring them here. You kidnapped us." I watched him walk into my cabin, as surefooted as if he trod on solid ground, staying upright despite the rocking boat. "Fine. Say your piece. It isn't anything I haven't heard before."

"Truly, Ember, I'm disappointed," he said. "I gave your friends ample opportunities to walk away, but they didn't. They needn't die alongside you."

I glared at him. "The funny thing is that when you lock someone in a cage and treat them like an animal, they don't tend to forgive and forget easily."

"And yet you walked so willingly back into the same cage."

"This doesn't look like a cage." I gestured to the cabin, resting my other hand on the wall to keep my balance. "Was this always your plan? Flee the country? I thought fighting the mages was your plan, not running away."

"The Mage Lords' time is coming to an end," he said. "We shall eliminate them in short order."

"I just saw you run away without confronting them." I

lifted my chin. "I think you're bullshitting. You're still too scared, aren't you?"

"Why would I offer them the advantage of engaging them on their own territory?" he queried. "No… their demise is in sight, but firstly, I must see to rectifying the vast amount of trouble your friends and yourself have caused me, Ember."

"I'm honoured." I gritted my teeth as the boat's rocking motion threatened to pitch me off the bed. "Pity you need me alive."

"Not any longer." His eyes glittered with satisfaction, or perhaps rage. "I have no need of a test subject for the time being, and any level of suffering you might endure isn't enough compensation for the damage you've inflicted. The hunters you've killed, the resources you've taken away, have created a blood debt which will never be repaid with mere suffering. Rather, your death will be a symbol that will have effects far beyond your own existence."

"A symbol?" I gave a snort. "Did you plan to mount my head on the wall outside your new base? Seems a waste if nobody knows where it is."

"Better." His smile widened. "Your body will be delivered to the Mage Lords, to prove that nobody alive can best us."

I choked on a disbelieving laugh. "The Mage Lords already hate me. They might even thank you for it."

"No." Now, his tone was deadly serious. "They will not, because your death will begin the next phase of our strategy to supplant the Mage Lords' authority."

"I thought you gave up on that goal." Of course he hadn't. The guy was a fanatic. If he didn't have the resources and the willpower to back up his overblown claims, I'd have dismissed him as a nutjob. "Should have figured warping shifters into your personal army wasn't enough for you."

"I did hope you met some of my new allies." His mouth lifted in a smile. "What did you think of them? Not every shifter reacted well to the alterations, but I've found that adaptation is the key to survival in this new world."

My stomach turned over, threatening to disgorge its meagre contents all over his shoes. "Is that why you turned yourself into a supernatural?"

"Don't be so crude. It's not possible to manufacture an aberration like you from a pure-blooded human."

"Oh, keep telling yourself that. You're a joke." My heart thudded in my ears, my shifter side striving to wake. "If you think you're sticking it to the mages by delivering my dead body to them, you're giving them what they want. They nearly killed me today already."

"Did they, now? I suppose it was a matter of time. You do have quite the habit of angering the authorities... or simply being in the wrong place at the wrong time."

"Is that a confession to starting the fire at Twill's shop?" I said. "Because you wanted to turn our neighbours against us?"

"You did that to yourselves, Ember, without any input from me. My hunters chose an appropriate way to dispose of the evidence. If that method drew your neighbours' suspicions... that says more about your conduct than mine, doesn't it?"

Evidence. He means the proof that the hunters stole the Moonbeam from Twill. I'd been right from the start. He *did* have the Moonbeam... but where?

"The mages aren't as oblivious to your activities in the city as you might think," I said. "If you show up to hand over my body, they'll kill you before you can utter a word."

"I hope you're not foolish enough to believe I would go there in person."

"No, that'd require you to have a spine." My body tensed at his dangerous expression, no longer laced with a mere trace of humour or the pretence of amiability. This man, I knew, would rip out *my* spine with his bare hands if the mood took him. He didn't even see me as a person.

At the same time, I knew that the Mage Lords would never willingly let the Orion League run around unchecked. Whatever he claimed, he must know that challenging every mage in London at once would risk destruction, and if their actual *leader* had taken notice of the League's operations, secrecy would soon be a distant memory. Moreover, the mages *were* more powerful, objectively, than the Elite soldiers. So were the faeries. The only way to play on a level field with supernaturals was to become one.

Or to create an army.

Those shifters. Where did he find them? Had the League been moving prisoners from the Stronghold for a long while, or had he snatched them off the street? Neither would surprise me, and the little I'd seen of the beasts he'd unleashed on London showed that they were as strong as several regular shifters put together. Maybe even enough to give the mages some major trouble.

Malkin lifted his head as if he'd heard something that I couldn't. "We're almost there."

"I can hardly wait." I dug my fingers into the wall as the boat gave another lurch. "You could have killed me in London if you wanted to make a statement, you know. This seems like a huge waste of everyone's time."

"The League's members deserve to witness your death, too," he said. "It's only right. Are you ready to come with me?"

No. Obviously, I wanted off the boat, but my arm and shoulder hurt like hell, and if an entire building full of hunters waited on the other side, I'd be hard-pressed to escape. I didn't know how long we'd been at sea, but we must be miles away from any semblance of civilisation.

Malkin left the room, and a pair of Elites took his place.

Try as I might, I still couldn't access my claws and could do nothing as the hunters cuffed my hands and feet together before dragging me across the deck.

Ahead lay our destination: an island, clouded with fog around a large fortress-like construction.

"This was disguised as a military base, back in the old world," Malkin said from behind me. "Impressive, isn't it? I'd advise you not to try anything, Ember. Your friends are counting on your cooperation."

My heart contracted. Ahead lay a stretch of concrete in front of the fortress. No greenery, and no other buildings. Just black-uniformed guards, masked Elites—and my friends, crouched on the ground with their hands and feet cuffed together. Will and Becks had turned human again, while Kit lay flat on his face as if he'd passed out cold. Given the iron cuffs, it was no wonder. A spasm of rage shook my body, but my claws still didn't emerge.

At the end of the group knelt Astor. His expression was as blank as I'd expected, but someone had beaten him, judging by the bruises on his face and the vicious red cuts visible through his torn shirt. *They're going to have him executed.* My friends, too. How was I supposed to save them all? Will could carry at least one of the others if he shifted, but the others had probably been hit by magic-nullifying darts, and Kit's handcuffs sapped his magic, so he might not even be able to use glamour.

Malkin directed the hunters to carry me to the other side of the concrete walkway, while more of them formed a line between us and the sea. I glimpsed more hunters gathering around the fortress and filing out of the doors in rigid lines. Ready to witness my death.

"Let's make this a little more interesting." He walked over to me, hauling me up by the scruff of my neck. I struggled and kicked, and the smell of decay and death washed over me as another group of hunters pushed an open crate off the boat and into the sea. The crate upended, spilling bloodied meat into the water.

Bait, I thought as I watched the hunters move in behind my friends and haul them to their feet. Everyone except Astor, who they gave a wide berth.

They weren't going to offer my allies the mercy of a quick death by bullet. Nor me, either. I squirmed, kicking out with my cuffed feet, but I couldn't break Malkin's grip while reduced to regular human strength. "What the fuck is this? If you feed me to the sea monsters, you won't have anything left of me to return to the mages."

"Oh, I think I'll let you watch your friends die first." He gestured to the fortress, where a pair of vast doors had opened. From within emerged several huge furred shifters like the ones that had attacked us before. "Kill them."

Astor moved, lunged at his captors. I didn't see what they did, but he immediately fell into a bloody heap at their feet.

Malkin sighed. "This really doesn't have to be so difficult for you, you know."

Red flickered across my vision. I jerked my head back, colliding with his chin. The blunt pain of hitting his shield reverberated through my body. With the platform trembling under the shifter beasts' weight, the vibration was strong enough for his hands to slip and send me plunging into the water.

19

For the second time that day, icy water flowed over my head, flooding my lungs. The metal cuffs seemed to drag me down, deeper into the abyss. The ocean was thick and relentless, and felt like swimming in dark soup. If I didn't drown, the beasts would have me first.

Is this how it all ends?

Under the surface, I couldn't hear the screams as my friends were ripped to shreds. All I heard was the ceaseless roar of the ocean as the salty water filled my mouth with the bitter taste of death.

Shift. Please, shift. I fought the current, kicking frantically, but I couldn't swim. I'd never learned how. Why would I, when dragons hated being wet, and water extinguished flame? My fists clenched under the handcuffs, but my hands refused to turn into claws. If Malkin wanted to present the Mage Lords with the head of a dragon, it looked as if he'd be disappointed.

A lone sound pierced the silence: the resounding *bang* of a bullet.

Someone's dead. One of my friends? God, I couldn't die

down here. A furious roar of pain burned my chest, unable to escape. My legs screamed in agony, each kick staving off death for a few more seconds. Raw pain and anger lapped inside me, and heat brewed in my chest. As my vision began to clear, a pair of lights pierced the darkness.

Not lights. Eyes, shining from within a mass of darkness. The two pinpricks shone above tentacles, parting around a gigantic pit-like mouth.

A grasping tentacle closed around my leg, and the rest of my held breath escaped in a scream. Panic and fear reached a crescendo and collided with my anger like a spark igniting. As I tugged, trying to free myself, my vision sharpened, my back arching as a growl ripped through my teeth.

Snarling, I tried to lift my claws, but the cuffs remained locked around my wrists. I'd thought I'd shifted, but my hands were still those of a human, unable to tear themselves out of the cuffs.

A stray tentacle whipped me across the face. My teeth tore through easily—a dragon's teeth—and I realised that it was my head that had shifted, not the rest of me. Spitting out the severed tentacle, I ducked my head, straining to reach the cuffs with my sharp teeth. My chest burned, my vision threatening to fade. I'd won myself a few precious seconds, but my human lungs were failing.

Amid the roaring darkness came the distinct *bang* of another shot.

The sound brought my shifter side to full wakefulness. Cuffs shattered as claws replaced my hands and feet, my wings extending from my back. When another tentacle enclosed my body, I clawed my way free, my dragon form more buoyant than I'd expected. With a strong kick, I broke the water's surface.

The cold, muggy air had never tasted so sweet. I inhaled, looked up to get my bearings. I'd drifted out from the island, but the line of hunters in front of the fortress remained, and animal screeches and growls echoed in my waterlogged ears. The sound of enraged shifters.

The hunters lined in front didn't seem to care for the danger, but Malkin must have ordered the shifters not to attack anyone but my friends. The question was, where were they? My heart lurched when I spied a body floating face-down. Blood fanned out, mingling with the murky water. *Astor.*

I kicked my way over to him, the momentum creating a wave that sprayed the hunters gathered on the platform's edge and forced several of them to break their formation. Uncaring, I lifted Astor in one claw. I couldn't tell whether he'd been shot, but he was bleeding badly and didn't seem to be breathing.

Voices shouted, Malkin amongst them, but I didn't stop to see where he was. I rose upward, whipping the sea with my tail, sending a fresh wave of water over the platform. Then I half flew, half swam to shore, Astor hanging from my claw. *He can't die here, not like this.*

I landed on the walkway, scanning the concrete surface. One of Malkin's shifter beasts lay dead, beyond the panicking hunters—but there was no sign of any of my friends. *Did Kit glamour them?* I'd thought the iron cuffs cut off access to his magic, but it was equally unlikely that Will or Becks had been able to shift and escape after being shot with suppressants that killed our supernatural powers.

A sharp *bang* prompted me to take flight. The hunters had snapped out of their shock at my reappearance and a dozen guns pointed at my head. I left the platform in a beat of my wings, but almost instantly, a heavy weight unbalanced me, pulled me down. A tentacle had grabbed my tail, intent on dragging me back into the deep.

"Take a hint," I growled, kicking at the beast, another shot whipping past my ear. As a dragon, I was too big a target.

I turned back into a human, and the weight pulling me down lifted as soon as my tail was gone. Three bullets whistled through the area where my wings had been as Astor and I hit the water. I was closer to the boat than the shore, so I grabbed Astor's arm and swam that way, gritting my teeth as sharp spasms of pain shot up my injured upper arm and shoulder.

When we reached the boat, I shoved Astor up onto the deck first and hauled myself after him, teeth chattering.

"She's on the boat," yelled Malkin from the walkway, where the sopping-wet crowd of hunters had swarmed, shouting over one another. "Bring her to me. This must end. I won't allow it."

The hunters surged towards the narrow plank connecting the boat to the walkway, abandoning all semblance of order in their effort to get to me. Or possibly to avoid the thrashing tentacles.

At my feet, Astor's eyelids flickered. *He's alive.* Had he been playing dead all along? As much as I wanted to ignore the hunters and give him a good shake for making me worry, a dozen or more guns pointed at us, and shifting would only make me into a bigger target again. My gaze skimmed over the hunters at the platform's edge, and the air flickered, revealing Will, Kit and Becks, crouched in the shadow of the fortress.

My heart lifted. They were alive. Somehow, they'd evaded the hunters' bullets and had slipped past the monstrous shifters under cover of Kit's glamour. How they'd pulled it off didn't matter. We weren't out of the game yet.

Several guns fired at once.

The first bullet travelled through the water's surface and hit me in the thigh. I hadn't registered the pain before the second hit my shoulder. I crumpled, hitting the deck beside Astor as a third bullet lodged itself in my upper arm.

It'd been so fast. So fast. My breaths came quickly as though my lungs knew they wouldn't have to work for much longer, my heart battering my ribs as if each beat might be the last… but I shouldn't have had time to notice that. Wasn't death from a hunter's bullet supposed to be almost instantaneous?

"That's her taken care of." Malkin snapped his fingers at the hunters. "Stop being so pathetic. It's only a little water."

"The others," said one of the hunters hesitantly. "They're hiding, with witchcraft."

"My security will sniff them out. They can't hide forever." Malkin extended a hand, revealing a fist-sized object as black as obsidian.

The Moonbeam.

A gasp caught in my throat. If he hadn't turned away to address the other hunters, I might have given myself away. As it was, I held as still as humanly possible as Malkin lifted the gleaming rock and called to the monstrous shifters gathered around the island. "Find them."

Heart racing, I bit the inside of my cheek to avoid making a sound as the hunters carried me back down the plank to the shore. I let my head and limbs hang limply, teeth gritted through each spasm of pain that jarred my injured arm. The hunters deposited me on the cold concrete, none too gently. They really did think I was dead.

Why didn't the bullets kill me?

Whatever miracle had spared my life, Malkin didn't know I lived. Astor, too, was alive, and the others were hidden, at least for as long as it took Malkin's monstrous shifters to sniff them out.

But Malkin had the Moonbeam. I couldn't leave the island without it.

I lifted my head, slowly, so as not to draw attention. Hunters stood all around me, reassembling at the railing overlooking the sea, and a strange rumbling sensation travelled through the concrete beneath.

The world tilted sideways, and I found myself sliding along the soaking concrete until I fetched up against the railing. Waves churned below, surging backwards and underneath the concrete as the rumbling noise gained a new familiarity. An engine. Like a boat… a massive one.

Holy shit. This isn't an island. It's like a huge battle station. A giant concrete-and-iron ship, heading for shore.

For London.

This was the hunters' endgame. The League was declaring war on the Mage Lords and bringing their army right into the heart of the city. Presenting them with my corpse would be a bonus, but my death hardly mattered when he had the Moonbeam in his grasp and a horde of monstrous shifters at his disposal. The mages wouldn't see the attack coming.

Unless I warned them first.

As the fortress rocked forward, I rolled over again, letting my body go limp. The railing caught me, but I was small enough in my human form that the gap underneath was narrow enough to fit through.

I rolled over again and slipped through the rails. A shout followed my descent into the water, into icy oblivion. Agony ignited in the bullet wounds, but fear dampened the pain, and I forced my head beneath the surface so that the hunters wouldn't see me moving under the dark waves.

Then I kicked, propelling myself through the deep, relying on the rumble of the moving fortress to work out my direction. Even as an inexpert swimmer with a bullet lodged in one leg, my shifter speed won out, and when I surfaced, I found I'd skirted the side of the fortress and left the hunters at the railing far behind.

I shifted into a dragon, using my wings to launch myself out of the water. The bullets cut a painful trail through my leg, arm and shoulder, but my dragon form could handle the pain better than I could as a human. Much harder was knowing that every wing beat took me further from my friends and the monstrous shifters trying to sniff out their hiding place. And Astor would have to draw upon every ounce of practise at impersonating a statue in order to fool the hunters into thinking him dead until he could escape.

I'll come back for you.

With wings, I could clear a vast distance in the space of minutes, and we were closer to the shore than I'd thought. Soon the silhouettes of high-rise buildings began to appear on the horizon, along with the narrowing mouth of the river. Another short stretch of time brought me close enough to properly see the skyline, and the gutted office blocks that now housed gargoyle street gangs.

Nearing the docks, I aimed for the warehouses where the mages had fought the gargoyles, but the sky was clear, and no lightning or fire pierced the air. They'd left.

Nothing for it. I'd have to fly directly to the mages' part of the city.

I kept both eyes open for low-flying gargoyles as I dipped beneath the clouds to figure out a landing spot. From above, London was a patchwork of tangled streets interspersed with patches of greenery. One of the larger green splotches was Hyde Park, which wasn't far from mage territory, so I headed that way, conscious that anyone who looked up at the sky would be able to see a giant red dragon.

Ah, well, I thought. *It's not like the hunters are planning to make a subtle entrance either.*

I dropped in height when I spotted the first group of individuals in long black cloaks walking near the park. None of them were from among the group who'd attacked us at the warehouses, but they'd have to do.

I dropped like a stone, landing in front of them. The man in front exclaimed, lifting a hand to display a swirling current like a miniature whirlpool. Of all the luck. "Don't move, dragon," he said warningly.

Oh, please. I could swat him like an insect, but the swirling current of water in his hand coupled with the blood dripping from my leg reminded me that fighting the mages would not work out in my favour. Besides, I'd come here to warn them.

I shifted into human form. My legs buckled as I did so, but I forced my hands to remain claws, just to give myself some protection. "I've come with a message for the Mage Lords," I said. "It's urgent. The hunters are coming to launch an attack on this city. They have—"

"She's the one Lord Smyth has us looking for," said one of the mages. "Bring her in."

20

The mages bundled me into a car and drove me through their neighbourhood at a speed that would never have been possible anywhere else in the city. The streets were in good enough condition that the invasion might never have touched them and were lined with expensive high street stores and restaurants. It was like driving through an alternate world where prestige and money had entirely kept the faeries away.

We turned down a side street, and the car parked around the back of a run-down building that stood in contrast to the mages' usual standards. This must be their jail for misbehaving supernaturals. Nice of them to give me the VIP treatment.

It took all my willpower not to fight back as they hauled me through a cramped reception area and into a corridor lined with cells. While the area didn't remotely resemble the Orion Stronghold in any other way, it was hard for my body not to react to the similarities. Sweat beaded my forehead, and my teeth rattled with my effort to suppress myself from shifting. Fighting wouldn't help, not now, and the lingering pain burning in my thigh and shoulder reminded me that the mages didn't have to unleash the full extent of their power to subdue me.

My captors deposited me on a narrow bench inside the cell with considerably less force than the hunters had used when they'd thrown me around. Even so, sudden weakness gripped my legs and threatened to send me into unconsciousness. Nobody seemed to have noticed I was injured.

I didn't know why I was still alive, but the three bullets must surely be causing some internal damage the longer they stayed lodged in my skin. Digging them out was out of the question without any weapons on me, and my claws were too big and cumbersome to use for a task that required finesse. It'd be a fine thing to accidentally bleed out when I was so close to the mages.

After only a few short minutes that nevertheless felt like an hour, footsteps came from outside. Lord Smyth entered the cell, looming over me with lightning crackling in his eyes that sent even my dragon side into retreat. One snap of his fingers, I knew, could summon a storm even my dragon form couldn't stand up to.

"Your name?" he said. "I don't believe I caught it earlier."

"It's Ember. The city is in danger. Please, you have to listen to me." I hated the weakness in my voice, but playing at surrender was my quickest route to cooperation. "The hunters are on their way to London. They've been hiding offshore in a fortress, and they have an army of shifters. Like the one who attacked us near the warehouses." I shifted my position to reveal the blood seeping down my shoulder and leg, but showing off the bullet holes wouldn't prove anything when I never should have survived one shot, let alone three.

Lord Smyth studied me. "We examined that shifter's body ourselves and found he was under the influence of some kind of magic we've yet to be able to identify. Is this something you can speak to?"

"I told you, it's the Moonbeam." Frustration bled into my voice. "I saw Malkin holding it with my own eyes. He and the hunters have been corrupting shifters and changing them against their will for the purposes of using them against—well, us. I don't know how many shifters they're bringing to the city, but it's a lot."

"The Moonbeam is a legend," he said. "There have been enough rumours to confirm its existence, I grant you, but nothing to prove that it has ever been in the League's possession."

"I told you, I saw it," I said impatiently. "Malkin told me plainly that he wants to replace you. I escaped his captivity to warn you, and I'd be happy to share more details if you agree to let me go."

"I'm afraid that bargaining is not an option for you, Ember." He studied my face again, as though searching for any trace of a lie. "Can anyone else back up your claims? Anyone who isn't a known criminal?"

"My friends can, but they're—still with the League." Guilt twisted into a knot in my chest. I might have been angrier with him for calling me a criminal if not for my certainty that I should have rescued them before I attempted to reason with the mages.

"Your friends are also wanted criminals. One even has a death sentence on his head. I'm afraid their word is no more reliable than yours is."

"He's already dead." Astor would want me to keep up the lie, and I'd gladly do so if it meant having an easier time making the mages see reason. "The League killed him for desertion, right before they tried to execute me so they could bring you my head as proof they can slay a dragon. That nobody can ever challenge them, including you."

"Really." He didn't believe me, but the sense of an imminent threat from him had dissipated. "I'll have to ask Lady Clare to verify that, and she's currently out on patrol."

Lady Clare. I recoiled inwardly at the thought of her probing into my thoughts, but how else to prove that I spoke the truth?

He retreated from my cell, pulling a mobile phone out of the pocket of his long cloak. Evidently, this part of the city didn't suffer from the signal issues that affected the rest of us ninety percent of the time. They probably had working internet and a steady supply of electricity, too. And what did they do with that advantage? Locked up innocent shifters and ignored the real threat on the brink of arriving on their doorstep.

Maybe I shouldn't have tried to help them at all.

Lost in sour thoughts, I lifted my head when my cell door clicked open again. This time Lady Clare came in, with Lord Smyth close behind.

Here we go.

"Read her," Lord Smyth told her. "She claims the Orion League is bringing an army to the city."

My head throbbed with pain the instant Lady Clare looked directly into my eyes. Thoughts flitted in and out of my mind as I recoiled away from exposing my inmost self to someone who hated me so deeply.

"Her mind isn't easy to penetrate," said Lady Clare. "She's already been tampered with, it seems."

"Tampered with?" My mouth went dry. How much had she seen?

"Someone used magic to affect your memories." Accusation layered her voice. "Or did you do it to yourself?"

"No." She must mean the memory spell, or whatever kind of magic had wiped out all recollection of my history before

I'd arrived in London. "You can see I'm telling the truth, though, right?"

"Lady Clare?" Lord Smyth looked questioningly at her. "Is it true? The League is coming to London."

"That does seem to be the case." Her gaze slid back to me again, eyes narrowing as if to pierce through to my deepest thoughts. The hint of a smile on her mouth, as if she *enjoyed* this, made me want to conjure up an imaginary brick wall bearing the words *fuck off.*

Anger tightened her mouth. Oops. Had she actually seen that? Lord Smyth stared at her questioningly, unknowing of the mental standoff that had passed between us.

"Is it true?" he asked. "The hunters are coming here with an army?"

"Yes. I saw a fortress heading for the river. And a boat." Her gaze cut from me to him, her mouth thinning into a line. "It's possible that she conjured the image to trick me. She's very strong-minded."

"I've never even met a mind mage before," I retaliated. "I wouldn't know how. And I can give you more."

I fixed the image of Malkin in my head, running through my mental recollections of him at his most depraved. Images played in my mind of Malkin taunting me in a cell, shooting the other dragon shifter dead, standing indifferently as the Elites shot at an unconscious Astor. When I threw in a mental image of the lab in which he'd been tormenting shifters and tacked that onto my memories of the shifter beasts roaming the island in search of my friends, she sucked in a sharp breath and looked away. "It's true. They're on their way here, all of them."

I didn't know how much of that she'd seen, but it must have been enough.

Lord Smyth took a startled step back. "How long do we have?"

"I don't know," I said. "Hours, maybe. It depends if they send any of their people ahead on boats, and how many of their shifters can fly."

The Mage Lord sucked in a breath. "Lady Clare, tell the other mages at once, and ask Lord Clyde to send a team to the docks."

"I can scout ahead and see how close they are," I offered. "In my dragon form, I can fly fast enough to head off their shifter army."

"You can't be serious," said another female voice from behind Lord Smyth. Apparently, we'd attracted an audience. "Lord Smyth, we can't trust the word of a criminal, and we certainly cannot accept her help."

"I didn't commit any crimes." Not that anyone was listening.

"Lady Clare is an accomplished mind mage," said Lord Smyth. "Nobody but a fellow mage would be able to fool her. Now, leave, all of you."

They did, including Lady Clare herself. Relief flooded me despite the grim certainty that if the hunters really did arrive in the city in a few hours, there was a depressing chance some of these people were going to die. When the others had cleared the room, I repeated my plea. "I can catch up to the hunters' army easily if I fly. I can't beat them all, but I can try to slow them down."

His brow furrowed as he considered me again. "Should your claims prove to be incorrect, I'm risking removal from my own position."

Does it matter? I bit back the words. It was just like a Mage Lord to be more worried about losing the respect of his fellow mages than an oncoming army. "I thought you trusted Lady Clare. I let her violate my privacy to prove my innocence, Lord Smyth, because it was the only way to convince you to listen before the hunters wiped all of you out."

"I can assure you that the outcome will not end in anything other than their own obliteration," he said, though his manner towards me had considerably warmed compared to earlier. "That said, we would appreciate any efforts to slow down the League's advance… that is, if I can trust you to submit yourself for questioning when this over. Your friends, too."

"I'll do that." *If we're both alive.* We both knew the danger the hunters posed, but he hadn't seen into my mind the way Lady Clare did, and I suspected that the mages were still underestimating how much of a danger Malkin posed.

Still, he'd offered me a lifeline. I'd be a fool not to take it. I got to my feet, my leg protesting as the bullet wound made itself known. My shoulder, too, burned with pain. "Ah. I don't suppose you have a healing spell?"

A frown appeared on his face. "You're injured. Apologies. I'll get you a spell at once."

Nice. The mages had access to the best healing remedies out there, though I still had no idea how I'd survived three of the hunters' bullets.

I accepted the healing spell and sighed in relief as my shoulder and leg stopped throbbing and the aches from my earlier bruises vanished, too. Then I followed Lord Smyth out of my cell and down the corridor to the entrance.

Since nobody said otherwise, I shifted straight into my dragon form the instant I was outside. With strong wing-beats, I cleared the rooftops until I hovered on a level with the lowest clouds. The Thames wound like a serpent below, choked with debris and the occasional boat. The hunters were nowhere in sight, but I could see the mages assembling on the docks near the warehouses.

I followed the river's curving line towards Tower Bridge and veered sharply to the side when I caught sight of a large winged shifter beast descending over the river. Malkin's shifters were already here. Hoping the mages were ready to meet them, I carried on flying until the open sea came within sight. Malkin must be out there somewhere, and through the fog smothering the ocean's surface, I spied a boat weaving its way through the water.

There he is. Inhaling, I released a stream of flame that nearly took the roof off the boat. As shouts came from the deck, I closed in, readied to burn the rest to cinders.

"Ember, you nutcase," roared Will. "It's us."

I flew lower, staring down at the deck. Will and Becks were in front, clinging to the railings. Nearby, Kit leaned over and vomited into the sea. I knew exactly how he felt.

They're alive. My friends were alive.

"It's a ghost dragon," said Will. "I didn't know that was a thing."

Kit lifted his head, his face almost as green as his eyes. "She's not a ghost. She's solid as we are."

"Yeah, she is." Becks peered up at me. "Unless she's undead?"

"Undead dragons can't breathe fire," Will said. "I don't think."

I laughed, the sound escaping as a booming roar that nearly made Kit fall into the sea. He clung onto the railing, half upside-down, as Will reached out to help him. *Oops.* I shifted back to human form and landed beside them, immediately sliding straight onto my back when the boat tipped sideways under my weight.

"I'm not dead." I looked up at the others. "I swear."

"Oh, thank god for that." Becks reached out and hauled me to my feet. "Don't you ever do that to us again, Ember. You'd better tell Astor, too. He's pissed off."

"Last I saw, he was doing a convincing job of playing dead himself." I grabbed the railing when the boat lurched forward as we hit a wave. "Who's driving this thing?"

"Astor." Will grabbed Kit and pulled him back from the railing before he fell.

I rolled my eyes. "Of course he can drive a boat."

"No, he can't," said Becks. "He's going to get us all killed."

"Did you steal this boat from the hunters while Malkin was commanding his shifter army?" I guessed.

"Yep. They're swimming with the fishes." Will grinned. "Not Malkin, unfortunately. He's in charge of that monstrosity behind us."

I couldn't see the fortress from this angle, but Malkin had already sent some of his army ahead, and it wouldn't be long before they caught us up.

"We need to get to London before that fortress does," I said. "Some of Malkin's winged shifter beasts are already there."

Becks swore as the boat hit a wave and went airborne for a good five seconds before crashing into the sea again, sending a spray of saltwater over the deck. Kit groaned, and I was glad I'd already thrown up everything I'd eaten in the past day.

Gripping the railing with a hand, I asked, "How'd you all get away?"

"Got lucky," Will said. "The dart they shot me with didn't go in properly, so I didn't get a full dose of the shifter suppressant crap. When they pushed you into the sea, my handcuffs broke when I shifted into gargoyle form, and I managed to break Kit's cuffs off, too. Then he used glamour on all three of us, and we hid until I was able to fly us off the island. Did you say the *Mage Lords* told you to come?"

"They caught me," I admitted. "I had to let one of them read my mind in order to prove I was telling the truth about the hunters coming to attack London."

"Damn," said Will, casting a worried look at Kit, who was retching into the ocean again. "You okay, Kit?"

"No." He whimpered. "I don't think I like boats as much as I like flying."

"He saved our necks back there," said Becks. "He hit the wolf shifters with some kind of spell that made them all confused. Oh yeah, and he healed all our injuries. Even Astor's."

"He can heal injuries?" I doubted Astor would have been pleased to have to subject himself to yet another form of magical influence, but it couldn't be helped.

"So can you," Becks said. "I swear I saw you get shot before you fell into the water. How are you still breathing?"

"I did get shot," I said. "Three times. Honestly, I don't know why I'm alive."

"That's down to me," said Astor. "I switched out the bullets."

All eyes turned towards him. He wore a smirk that caused my dragon side to stir with interest, even with both of us covered in blood and dirt from the filthy ocean water.

"What?" Will gaped at him. "When on earth did you have time to do that?"

"While you were riding in the truck, I sneaked up on the hunters at the docks and switched their weapons for ones with harmless bullets designed to disintegrate on contact with minimal damage," he said. "Giselle has enough spare guns that I carried some myself in the hopes that they'd confiscate them from me if I got caught. It didn't even cross their minds that they weren't the real deal."

"Damn," said Becks. "That's sneaky."

"It is." *Wait a moment.* "Aren't you supposed to be driving the boat?"

"I assumed we'd be flying. Frankly, I'd prefer that option."

So would I, but flying back to the city would bring us all within reach of the mages. Including Astor. They'd agreed to spare my friends' lives, but not his.

Tentacles lashed at the deck. The boat rocked left and right, buffeted by the beast below. Had it followed the boat?

"Damn." I caught the railing as we hit another wave. "Guess I made it angry."

"What the fuck *is* that?" said Becks.

"Kraken, I think." I shifted my hands to claws and swiped at an oncoming tentacle as Will shifted into gargoyle form to avoid being yanked off his feet.

Green light flashed, and the kraken recoiled, its tentacles withdrawing. The faerie held his hands aloft and fired another bolt of green light at the beast, and even Astor almost looked impressed at the display.

Another tentacle slammed into the boat's right-hand side, while more rose from the waves on the left. Damn, that monster was bigger than I'd realised. As another wave hit the deck, Becks shifted into cat form and dug her claws into the floor, her fur standing on end from the soaking.

"We don't have time for this." I lifted my clawed hands. "Nobody else is on board, are they?"

"No," growled Astor, grabbing at me as we both skidded across the deck. "Does it matter?"

"Yes, because I'm planning to set it on fire. Ready, Will?"

I shifted into dragon form and grabbed Astor in my claw before he could voice an objection. A moment later, Will took flight with Kit clinging to his back and Becks on top, her claws digging into the half-faerie's shoulder. With everyone clear, I took aim.

Despite the salt taste in my mouth, the fire came as naturally as ever, a stream of flames that swiftly engulfed the boat in a plume of orange-white. *Bye, bye, kraken.*

"Dramatic," said Astor, dangling from my claw. "Damn, woman, put me on your back."

"Scared, Astor?" The words came out as a growl, but the glare he shot at me made me wonder if I was more intelligible as a dragon than I'd thought. That, or Astor was just unusually perceptive. Still, it couldn't be comfortable dangling from my claw, so I placed him between my wings and flew on.

Soon we closed in on Tower Bridge. Screams reached my ears from below, where winged shifters dive-bombed people on the banks. As I veered that way, lightning arced down from the sky, knocking one of the beasts straight out of the air. Good, the mages were here. Hoping they didn't look up and see Astor on my back, I continued to fly above the river, occasionally exhaling a stream of flame to warn away any winged shifters in my path.

Past the bridge, the mages gathered on both sides of the river to face the attacking shifters. More fought on the ground, near the place where the boat had been docked earlier. Not against shifters but against humans. Elites, from the look of their uniforms and weapons. They must have stayed in the city while the boats left.

The mages met them blow for blow, throwing fire and ice, lightning and wind, but they'd clearly been taken by surprise as much as anyone else. I swooped down, grabbed two Elites and threw them into the river, but I didn't dare linger too close to the ground in case the mages saw Astor.

I could hear him swearing on my back as I gained speed, heading for the warehouses. A gargoyle appeared in my flight path, suddenly enough that our collision knocked me off course. I spiralled downward and caught my balance above a warehouse roof.

Astor swore loudly. "There's a dozen gargoyles down there. Change course!"

"What—?" My growl cut off in a huff of disbelief. Gargoyles filled the space above the warehouses, seemingly oblivious to the fight that had broken out on the riverside, and entirely blocking my escape route.

21

A rumbling growl arose amid the gargoyles as they circled me, reacting to a fellow predator. I glared at them, projecting all the fury I could muster. Astor's words from a few days ago trickled through my mind.

Clearly, Ember wasn't affected because she belongs to the same class of shifter as the beast. When I'd first shifted in front of my friends, they'd claimed to have been paralysed, unable to move.

I drew upon my anger and directed it straight at the gargoyles, releasing a roar that rattled the warehouse roofs. Some of them recoiled, but the majority merely watched me, blank-eyed, as if my mere presence had turned them to the stone they already resembled. A shiver trailed over my back.

A whirring noise broke the silence. Astor leaned forward and hissed, "Ember, it's him."

Malkin. A small helicopter appeared in my peripheral vision, Malkin himself seated in front. He appeared to be flying the helicopter himself. As he landed on a warehouse roof, the whirring died down. He'd left his army behind, but when he climbed out, he lifted a palm, displaying the Moonbeam.

"Let me kill him," growled Astor. "I don't need a weapon. I can push him off the roof with my bare hands."

I doubted he'd even get close. The Moonbeam gave Malkin total control over the surrounding gargoyles, and if he used it on me, too…

I had to strike first. Fire seared my chest, and I looked directly into his eyes with all the power I'd unleashed against the gargoyles. *Freeze, you bastard.*

Malkin regarded me with calmness, as though I'd had no effect on him whatsoever. Did the Moonbeam protect him, or some other side effect of the magical tattoos he'd inked on himself?

Give me the Moonbeam. I growled, low and menacing, making my meaning as clear as possible. *That's mine.*

"You're a remarkable creature, aren't you?" Malkin looked me over, his expression almost approving. "I can't help but admire your effort in evading me, heedless of the cost to yourself and your allies."

"Neither of us wants to listen to you, Malkin." As I flew lower, Astor leaped from my back to land in front of him on the roof.

"Number three oh eight," said Malkin in tones as cold as the ocean he'd thrown me into. "You're of no interest to me whatsoever."

He lifted the Moonbeam. A jet of pure white light shot from the stone, and a nearby gargoyle broke free of my spell and dove at Astor.

I flew up to meet it, grabbing the struggling gargoyle by the wing before its claws reached Astor. Though my instincts urged me to rip out its throat, my desire to keep Astor and Malkin in my field of vision stayed my hand.

"Strange," said Malkin. "Very strange, for the pair of you

to risk so much for one another when you are enemies to the core. I assume you're the reason she survived being shot, too?"

Astor reached to his belt for a knife and threw it at Malkin. The knife spun once—but bounced clean off an invisible shield before it made contact with Malkin's hand. As the knife toppled out of sight, the Moonbeam flashed again, and two more gargoyles swooped upon the roof behind Astor.

"A pointless exercise," Malkin said softly. "For both of you to come here… I confess I hoped to confront Ember alone, but I do expect I'll find a use for both of you."

"Keep talking." I growled the words, my gaze fixed on the glowing stone in his hand. If Astor had been able to make him drop it, I might have stood a chance at snatching it for myself—if not for Malkin's protective spells rendering even my fire incapable of touching him.

"I knew you would be unable to resist the Moonbeam's allure, even while free from its influence." He held the Moon-beam aloft. "It's astonishing, in a way, that a mere stone is able to exert such an effect on beings that possess so much power of their own. Certainly, it is further proof that you are nothing but animals at heart, a corruption threatening to infect the rest of humanity."

A growl slid through my teeth, and my claws bit deeper into the gargoyle I held by the wing. I didn't know whether Astor had a plan or if he'd hoped I'd strike while Malkin's attention was split, but my freedom would last only as long as Malkin didn't use that stone on me, like he had the gargoyles.

"How many times have you used that artefact to stage shifter attacks on humans?" Astor said quietly. "Nearly every recruit who stayed in the League long enough to reach the higher ranks was the survivor of a shifter attack. That's no coincidence."

Was that true? I knew that Astor himself had lost his family to a dragon shifter, that the League often chose recruits with a similar background, but everyone knew that even among shifters who lived in the wild and shunned human customs, it was very rare for one to attack someone unprovoked.

Dread sank deep roots in my chest. The Moonbeam allowed the person who held it to wield total control over any shifter. Had he used it to manipulate the other dragons, too? Was *he* the reason they had a reputation as bloodthirsty monsters?

"Tell me the truth, you bastard," said Astor. "Did you order a shifter to kill my family?"

Malkin ignored him, but he didn't need to say a word when the absence of denial spoke for itself. White-hot rage rose, ignited the fire in my chest.

As I took aim at Malkin, he lifted his gaze to me. "Kill him."

The fire died in my throat, my mind blanked, and a glorious calm settled over me as the turmoil in my heart stilled. Rather than breathing fire at Malkin, I released the gargoyle and dove at the rooftop, readied to grab Astor and rip off his head.

Astor threw himself down, and my claws scraped the roof's flat surface as he rolled over, dodging me with shifter-worthy speed. I snagged the back of his coat with my claw and flung him aside, like a cat playing with a toy mouse. Never mind the gargoyles, never mind the man watching us. I had to kill him.

Astor dodged my claws for a second time, crawling through my front legs. A growl of frustration built in my chest at the audacity of a tiny human getting out of my reach. I was a predator, and he was nothing more than an ant.

On his feet, he skirted the edge of the roof as he dodged blow after blow. Finally, the edge of my claw caught him in the face. My claw shot out and caught him around the waist before he fell. Watching him fall to his death wouldn't be nearly as fun as taking him to pieces myself—but when I placed him on the roof, he jumped off.

A frustrated roar escaped. I reached to catch him, and he slid through my grip and crashed into a pile of empty crates. The impact must have hurt, but he was alive somewhere in there. Snarling in frustration, I dove down, clawing, biting, tearing at the crates in an attempt to extract him. I saw him hiding behind a crate and ripped it aside, leaving him exposed. *There you are.*

"Ember!" growled Astor. "Turn human again, damn you. I thought we already went through this."

Inexplicably, his words trickled through the command lodged in my mind. With the bright light of the Moonbeam no longer shining, my mind was fuzzier, less certain.

"Have you forgotten?" His voice dropped to a low purr. "Remember the net?"

A memory jolted into the forefront of my mind. The two of us at a stalemate on Magic Avenue, a net binding my wings to my back.

"Bastard." The word came out as a growl, but the desire to incinerate him began to lift.

He didn't take his eyes off me as he reached out a hand, rested a palm on my claw. Unafraid. He never had feared me, I realised, not since the moment he'd realised the human and dragon were one being.

"Come back, Ember," he said. "Or we'll never get to finish our conversation the other night."

Another memory of the pair of us poised on a roof,

locked together in mutual desire. I stumbled on human legs, and when he caught my arm, I fastened my lips to his and gave in to the new fire roaring through my veins, consuming every other instinct.

Astor shoved at my shoulders, breaking the kiss. "Ember, Malkin's on the roof. We need to kill him."

I blinked, mind still fuzzy. "What?"

"Malkin," said Astor. "Up there. Alive. With the Moonbeam."

Shock punched me in the chest, as if I'd fallen into the river all over again. My sense of self returned as swiftly as it had retreated when the light had taken away my will. "I can't shift. Not if he's going to… do that again."

"Neither can I, little dragon. Improvise."

"Damn you." I struggled to marshal my scrambled thoughts. The Moonbeam… that was the crux of everything. "We need to get it out of his hand. If not for that shield of his—"

"On it." He gestured to a small dart gun at his belt.

A grin stole onto my face. "I knew you wouldn't have got away without stealing one of those."

"I've learned to never let an opportunity go to waste."

I let my claws slide out. "Let me climb up first. If he uses the Moonbeam on me before I can kill him, get the hell off the roof and run."

I reached for the wall, my claw digging gouges into the metal sheeting as I scaled the warehouse. Astor climbed with the ease born of years climbing across rooftops. I wished he'd stayed on the ground, but he'd have to be high up in order to take aim.

Malkin showed no surprise at my reappearance. "Have you not learned that you can't touch me, Ember?"

It's not me you should be worried about, I thought. Out of the corner of my eye, Astor reached the rooftop behind me and went for the dart gun.

There came the sound of a dozen pairs of wings descending, and a moment later he was pinned under the weight of a gargoyle's claws.

"I'm surprised that you'd be so careless with your friends' lives," Malkin added. "I know your sister is *very* dear to you, and it must hurt very much that I hold the only means of saving her in my hands."

I said nothing. One eye dropped to Astor, who hadn't managed to grab the gun before the gargoyle had landed on his back. One flick of its claw would end him.

"I might have thought you'd try to negotiate," Malkin went on. "Perhaps that's too much to expect from the intellect of a mere animal, but I admit I very much dislike unfinished business. So, you're going to tell me where your sister is, or I will order the gargoyles to tear the traitor to pieces."

"You'll do it anyway, you scumbag." He wouldn't spare Cori, either, not when he'd all but confirmed he didn't need a captive dragon shifter as a lab rat any longer.

There came a muffled blast from somewhere below, shaking the warehouse roof. I lost my balance and slid onto my back, digging in my claws to keep from falling.

The gargoyle took flight, unbalanced, and Astor rolled over the edge. As he began to fall, another, smaller gargoyle flew underneath, catching Astor in mid-air. *Was that Will?* The gargoyle was gone before I could confirm its identity, but with Malkin's focus briefly elsewhere, I launched myself at him.

As expected, I collided with an invisible shield and found myself flung back onto the roof before my hand could close around the gleaming black rock.

Worth a try. I pushed to my knees, a sudden burst of light dazzling my eyes. The Moonbeam was glowing, but my head was clear. A faint vibration seemed to emanate from the stone, quiet enough that I felt more than heard it, thrumming under my skin like a pulse.

Malkin might be able to use the Moonbeam, but he wasn't one of us. He couldn't understand an item that had been made for shifters alone. The fire in my chest rumbled to life, the vibration in sync with the beat emanating from the Moonbeam.

"I wouldn't, Ember." Malkin reached for his belt with his free hand and lifted a gleaming gun to point at me. "I know all about your people, Ember. The Moonbeam illuminates all, and it will ensure that no dragon shifter ever stands against me again."

His finger hovered over the trigger. I suspected that I was hoping for too much if I thought Astor would have had the chance to switch out *his* bullets with fake ones. Malkin would never have let him get that close.

"Tell me where your sister is, Ember, or I will tear this city from the roots to find her," he said. "The lives of all the people in London are in your hands. I hope you'll choose wisely."

22

As I stared into the barrel of Malkin's gun, all I could think was *It's over. We've lost.*

No. I wouldn't accept that. As long as my lungs drew breath, I would fight on, for myself and for my friends. And for Cori.

"How do you even know how to use the Moonbeam?" I asked him, stalling for time. "It belongs to the dragon shifters."

"How do you think?" A smile nudged at his lips. "Your fellow unnaturals can be quite cooperative, given the right incentive."

Anger bloomed. He'd likely tortured the information from his former captive. Was there no end to his cruelty?

"And you still expect me to give up Cori."

"Oh, I don't, but I do wonder if your loyalty to a sister who's already on the brink of death should be your priority when I can offer you far more. Wouldn't you like to know how to find the rest of your kind?"

His words struck somewhere deep within, but I forced

myself to speak calmly. "No, because every word that comes out of your mouth is a lie."

I didn't believe him. He'd never give me that information unless he knew I'd never be able to use it to my advantage. And I had no intention of being pushed to that point.

"You can still spare the rest of the city," he went on. "That part wasn't a lie. I have little desire to be responsible for the mass slaughter of innocent humans who played no part in the unnaturals' usurpation of their home."

"Every time you come close to making sense, you end up disappointing me." I did my best imitation of his patronising tone. "The supernaturals didn't ask to be invaded either, any more than we asked for the League to try to exterminate us."

"It was your presence that turned this realm into a target." He gestured at the sky, at the gargoyles amassing around the warehouses, and at the shifter beasts in the distance, doing battle with the mages on the ground. "The Mage Lords' supremacy ends today."

Through gaps amid the gargoyles, I glimpsed fiery clouds and flashes of lightning, signs of the mages' ongoing fight. And—Astor, seated on a gargoyle's back, hidden amid the others. How on earth had Will persuaded him to ride on him? *Right, I have to survive this, if only to ask.*

I turned my eyes back to Malkin's face before he realised one of the gargoyles present was not under the Moonbeam's thrall. "You think defeating London's mages in a single battle will win you victory over every supernatural in the world?"

That was assuming the mages had lost. From the flashes of lightning still igniting the sky, the mages were giving as good as they got. They might be flawed in a thousand ways, but they knew better than to surrender to the likes of Malkin. And so did I.

"Humans once ruled this world," he said. "They—and we

—outnumber the unnaturals as a collective, and soon we will regain supremacy with no magical blood to corrupt us."

"You're already corrupt."

My sharp ears picked up on a pinging sound, and Malkin looked down in surprise at the dart embedded in his hand.

The same hand that held the Moonbeam.

As the stone began to ignite, I lunged at Malkin in a wild movement that sent us both over the edge. The gleam of the Moonbeam caught my eye, sliding from Malkin's limp hand.

He grabbed for it, missed, and I shifted into dragon form. My claw closed around the Moonbeam, and my wings beat once, carrying me out of Malkin's reach.

Then I breathed dragonfire.

The fireball hit the warehouse on which Malkin had stood, scorching the roof to cinders and causing the nearby gargoyles to rise in the air with cries of terror. A cloud of dust exploded outward as the building collapsed in on itself. A second blast of fire sent the gargoyles scattering, and a shout drew my attention to Astor waving at me from Will's back.

"Get out of here," I tried to growl at them. "Go and find the others."

Where were Kit and Becks? Safely out of range, I hoped. As I flew closer, Will detached himself from the other gargoyles, Astor leaning over his shoulder.

"You have it," he said. "Can you stop them?"

That's the plan. If I could figure out how to use it. I needed to find somewhere open to land, so I flew past the warehouses towards the waterfront.

Mages and shifter beasts did battle, forks of lightning and fireballs splitting the sky in turns. On the ground, I spied Kit and Becks fighting off one of the non-winged shifters, surrounded by a shimmering green shield that prevented the monsters from landing a hit on them. Nearby, several hunters' corpses floated in the river, blood mingling with the murky water.

When I landed in front of my friends, I turned human again. "Are you all right? The fortress…"

"It's not here yet, but half the army is." Becks flinched as a lightning bolt hit the building behind us. "And the mages aren't paying all that much attention to collateral damage."

"It's okay." I held up the Moonbeam, and her eyes widened. "I'll handle it, once I figure out how this thing works."

I turned the gleaming stone over in my hand, sensing the same faint vibration under the surface that I'd picked up on earlier. Above, one of the winged beasts began to descend, claws splayed, and I lifted the stone to display its gleaming surface.

"Go," I said. "You can still save yourselves. Stop attacking us."

The beast continued its descent, but I held the stone higher, tightening my grip until its vibration hummed through my hand, my arm, my whole body. A resonance within my very blood and bones.

The Moonbeam's glow brightened, reflected in the shifter's eyes as its path changed and its feet landed harmlessly upon the ground.

"Stop," I murmured. "You remember how to be human."

As the light faded, the beast shrank back into the form of a human man. He keeled over, perhaps in shock, but I didn't have time to check on him with countless others to save from Malkin's thrall. I lifted my gaze to the sky, momentarily overwhelmed at the sheer number of winged beasts soaring over the river. That wasn't counting the ones on the ground, but to reach them all, I'd need to fly straight into range of the mages' attacks.

Will landed behind us, Astor sliding from his back. "What are you going to do?"

"Stop the army." I faced the river and the mages battling on the shore. "You guys stay out of range. I'll be back."

I ran, through the melee, holding the Moonbeam high so that its light drew the eyes of everyone who passed within my range of vision. One of them threw a fireball at me, which I dodged, shouting, "Hey! I'm here to save you."

Reaching the riverside, I shifted into dragon form and took flight with the Moonbeam securely locked in my grip. Its glow was even more mesmerising as a dragon, and the vibration hummed in sync with the fire brewing in my chest. Facing the oncoming shifters heading for shore, I growled, *"Leave. Turn human again. Give up."*

And they did. As one, they flew in retreat. Some landed at the riverside, others disappearing amid the city buildings and more still soaring away in all directions until the air was thick with the rhythm of beating wings.

Gradually the mages' attacks died down as they realised their adversaries had gone, though that didn't stop the fire mage from taking another shot at me as I descended near the pier.

"You ungrateful bastards," Astor shouted. "She saved your necks."

I felt oddly flattered. The fireball had barely tickled me, but I had to clear this up.

I landed, shifted into human form, and addressed the mages. "I'm on a mission for Lord Smyth. We all are."

And he'd better be bloody grateful for it.

Once I'd ensured they weren't about to take aim at my friends, I took to the sky again and followed the river's course. It didn't entirely come as a surprise when I reached the river's opening and found no sign of the vast island-fortress within my field of vision. Malkin—if he'd survived—would have ordered the army to change course as soon as he knew I had the Moonbeam and could stop any shifter he sent at me.

While I didn't believe for an instant that he'd died when the warehouse had collapsed, my real purpose for getting my hands on the Moonbeam was to save my sister. All I needed was to hear her voice again, and everything we'd gone through would be worth it.

———

"It's gone," I said to Lord Smyth. "The Moonbeam. Malkin dropped it when I breathed fire at the warehouse, and I didn't see if it survived."

"You didn't search for it afterwards?" The scepticism in his tone made it clear he didn't entirely believe me, but it wasn't like I had the Moonbeam in my pocket. Astor had taken it straight back to Giselle's house while I stayed behind to fulfil my side of the agreement with Lord Smyth.

"I tried," I said. "It was gone, and so was Malkin. I'm not convinced he died, though. Astor shot him with a dart that suppressed whatever abilities he gave himself, but he's escaped certain death once before."

"At the Orion Stronghold." I'd given him the whole story, or most of it, as soon as I'd submitted to being questioned. This time he'd brought me to the mages' main headquarters, a manor house with enough rooms to host the entirety of London's gargoyle shifter population and still have room for visiting dignitaries from the human government. The mages truly inhabited a different world to the rest of us mere mortals.

"Yes," I replied, fidgeting in the high-backed seat. It wasn't an interrogation, exactly—the office was too homely for that, the walls decorated with portraits of past Mage Lords and the plush carpet soft enough that I was tempted to curl up on the floor and go to sleep—but I'd been here for close to two hours and wanted nothing more than to go back to my sister. To wake her up, at long last.

I hadn't told the mages that she was in a coma and needed the Moonbeam to wake her, and I'd kept the details of our current hiding place to a minimum, making out that we were hiding off-grid in a shifter-run safe house. Luckily, he hadn't brought in Lady Clare to verify my every claim. In the aftermath of the battle, my word was enough, for now. He seemed to trust me. For a wonder.

Except on one matter. "It seems to me that if Malkin did escape, with the Moonbeam, we can expect a similar attack again in a short time."

"He's injured." Assuming he'd even survived, but I didn't believe for a minute he'd have been without a backup plan or three. "And we wiped out enough of his army to give him a good scare. Also, now he knows the mages will fight back if he challenges them."

His eyes narrowed a little, as if he'd picked up on the unspoken implication that this was the first time the mages *had* demonstrated any interest in fighting the League. "We will certainly be combing the city for him. Are you absolutely certain the Moonbeam didn't make it back to your friends?"

"Yeah." I bit my lip. "You really didn't know the League had it?"

"No," he said. "It's an object of legend, in truth, and one that the mages never had cause to take an interest in."

I bet they didn't. It belonged to the shifters—and I'd make damn sure it stayed that way. "All right. I've told you everything I know, and I'd really like to go home. My sister is probably frantic with worry."

Lord Smyth's expression softened, as I'd planned. It was an underhanded move considering I'd blatantly lied to him, but I was so damn tired, and I didn't want to alienate the mages by speaking my mind. While I didn't agree with all their methods, we needed to work together if we wanted to prevent the League from launching another attack. And there'd be one coming, I had no doubt.

"First we have to talk of your reward," he said. When I blinked, he added, "Why the surprise? You helped the Mage Lords, and we would not allow that to go without compensation. Do you have any requests?"

Damn. What did I want? "I want my sister and me to stay safe. We had to leave our jobs and go into hiding because the gargoyles attacked our house, thinking we killed some of their people. We didn't. It was the hunters. Also, I'd appreciate it if the mercenaries would stop asking for everyone to officially register for ID that exposes us as supernaturals. The same goes for whoever sent letters to everyone on Magic Avenue." Added together, it sounded like a lot, but the mages could literally move mountains if they wanted to.

"I will endeavour to fulfil your requests." A hint of hardness entered his expression. "You should know that your rewards will be delivered on one condition."

I looked at him warily. "Yes?"

"Hand over the hunter. We know he's not dead."

———

"IN CONCLUSION, MAGES ARE WANKERS," said Will. "I can't believe the bastard offered you everything you wanted only to snatch it away because you won't give up Astor."

"Yeah." I half-lay on Giselle's living room floor, exhausted beyond words. I'd flown back here in dragon form as soon as the mages had let me go, having to avoid three groups of gargoyles in the process, and delivered the bad news. "As if it was even a question."

Astor himself stood in the corner, the only one of us who hadn't collapsed onto the floor as soon as we'd got in the house. "They never would have given you what you wanted. The mages are too set in their traditions to meddle in shifter business, and I expect Lord Smyth is facing a lot of scrutiny from outside the city for letting you walk free."

"Coming from the guy who used to *work* for them," said Becks. "I bet that's what their problem is. They're embarrassed not to have noticed."

"That's probably part of it, but they also really wanted that Moonbeam," Astor put in. "If that mind-reading mage gets too close a look at Ember..."

"She can have it *after* I use it on Cori." What with checking one another for injuries and giving the others a rundown of the grilling the mages had given me, I had yet to even pull the Moonbeam out of my rucksack. "It's not like I can tell them how to use it."

"Are you sure Malkin won't just steal it back?" said Will. "I mean, the mages aren't known for paying attention to what's right under their noses."

Giselle scoffed from the sofa, her only contribution so far. Otherwise, it was clear that this would be our last day in her hideout. With the hunters gone, we'd go back to Magic Avenue and try to rebuild from there. Hopefully without having to put our names on any registers. The Mage Lords had never wanted that, I was sure, but I didn't trust them not to keep tabs on us in their own way. And lying to them indefinitely was impossible when one of them could read minds.

Though my previous encounter with Lady Clare did raise a question: namely, had a mage been the one to erase mine and Cori's memories before we'd arrived in London? I doubted London's mages could give me answers on that one, so I filed it away for later.

It was past time I got my baby sister back.

As I reached into my rucksack, the back door closed, telling me that Giselle had gone outside. I rummaged around then tipped the bag upside-down.

The Moonbeam was gone.

A loud bang from outside had us all on our feet. "What the hell was that?"

"One of our guns." Astor ran for the door, and I was right behind him as we emerged into the back garden.

Giselle stood next to the ruined fence with a gun in her hand and the Moonbeam lying at her feet in the grass.

"Did you *shoot* it?" I said, stunned. "What the fuck are you doing?"

"I'm going to destroy it," she said. "Before you're foolish enough to hand it over to the mages."

"I need to save my sister, remember?" She'd lost it. Her eyes gleamed manically, her hand shaking on the gun's trigger. Luckily, the Moonbeam itself didn't have so much as a dent in it. "Give it back. What the hell is the problem?"

"You have no idea what this object is capable of, Ember," she said. "The army that attacked London is the least of what Malkin will do if he gets his hands on this again."

"I'm not planning on letting him near it."

The door opened wider as the others came out of the house behind me, but I'd had too many shots fired at me to turn my back on Giselle when she had a gun in her hand and intended to use it.

"You've already proven that you're willing to compromise anyone and anything to protect your allies," said Giselle. "I won't have it."

"Let me save my sister," I repeated. "That's all I want."

"And then you'll let it go, when it can potentially help you find your fellow dragon shifters?" She gave a harsh laugh. "I know you better than that, Ember. You don't know what evil this object has inflicted."

"I do. Malkin told me." I really *didn't* want to get into that discussion right now. Astor had already worked out that Malkin had staged the attack on his family, but it had slipped my mind that the same must be true of Giselle, and of countless other League members, too. Had Astor told her? Or had she worked it out on her own?

Was that why she'd stolen the Moonbeam in the first place?

A glint appeared in her eyes. "And you still won't allow me to destroy it."

"I'm not sure it *can* be destroyed." Could even a supernatural-killing bullet take out the Moonbeam? "And no, I won't let you destroy it *before I save my sister.* That's the only reason we're still here at your house. Once you let me wake her up, we're out of here, and you never have to see us again."

"Giselle," said Astor in a low voice. "Be reasonable. Ember doesn't want any of the power the Moonbeam can offer. Malkin might not even have survived."

"You don't believe that, Astor. None of you do. He's alive, and he wants it back."

"You can do what you like, *after* I save Cori. That was the whole point in all this. Not power, or—or even finding the other dragon shifters."

Giselle, though? It was plain that she'd only told me about the Moonbeam because she wanted it destroyed, not out of any desire to help us. And while I'd known I'd pissed her off by risking her house being discovered, I never would have thought she'd stand between me and Cori.

She lowered the gun. "I'll do it myself."

I held my breath as she picked up the Moonbeam, an expression of revulsion on her face as if she was handling a dead animal. She entered the house, the gun held in a loose grip. I was tempted to kick it out of her hand, but I didn't need to start another fight.

Save Cori. Deal with the unhinged ex-hunter later.

Cori lay in her usual spot, prone on the mattress, unaware of the chaos unfolding around her. Giselle hobbled over to her and held out the Moonbeam. "What am I supposed to do with this?"

"I think only a shifter can use it," said Becks uncertainly. "Give it back to Ember. She's the expert."

"Hardly." Giselle's gaze travelled over all of us. Kit looked terrified, Becks looked angry, and even Will didn't make one of his usual flippant remarks. "I don't trust any of you."

"Ouch," said Will. "Really, I think Ember might be the only one who can use it. She's the only one who's tried, anyway."

"You do it." Giselle threw the Moonbeam at Will, who caught it by his fingertips. Then she pressed the gun to my back and yanked me roughly away from Cori. "Don't touch it."

"This isn't necessary," said Astor. "Nobody here is working against you, Giselle. You're wrapped in old paranoia."

"With cause," said Giselle. "You forget who's hunting us."

"I'm perfectly aware," Astor said in a low, dangerous voice. "We just fought a battle against them for the sake of that Moonbeam, and you might at least let Ember use it for its intended purpose."

"Intended purpose," spat Giselle. "What a joke. It never should have existed."

Will raised an eyebrow, but when I gave him an encouraging nod, he crouched down beside Cori. The Moonbeam glowed faintly in his palm. "How do I use it? Wave it around? Do an interpretive dance?"

"If you so much as move from that spot, I'll destroy it," said Giselle. "You're a shifter, aren't you?"

"And you're out of order." But he lifted Cori's hand and curled her fingers around the stone. "This is all I can think of."

For an instant, nothing happened. Then gradually, the stone's glow grew brighter, whitening to the same sheen as dragonfire.

"Aha," Will said triumphantly. "It's working."

"You can't know that," said Kit, edging away from Giselle. "Is nobody going to mention she's pointing a gun at us?"

The glow intensified until I had to look away, my eyes squinting. Then—

"Huh?" said a faint voice. "Oh. Hi, Will. Where am I?"

"Cori." Ignoring Giselle, I practically flew to my sister's side. Cori sat up on the mattress, looking down at the stone in her hand.

"Huh." She turned it over, examining the shiny surface. "What's this?"

"Put it down—" My warning cut off in a yelp as the light blazed so brightly that I thought for a moment that it had blinded me. Dazzled, I squinted, trying to make out the others amid the blur of light and colour. The Moonbeam's light had extended to cover a large section of the wall behind Cori, like sunlight spilling through an open window.

Cori dropped it with a cry of shock, and Giselle gave a lunge. I got into the way, and both of us fell sprawling onto the floor, Giselle's hand reaching towards the stone. Its halo kept on expanding, like a bright shadow, forming an angular shape that resembled a large pane of glass, or a mirror.

Giselle pushed upright—treading on my face in the process—and gave another grab for the Moonbeam. Her hand went *through* the surface of the stone, through the white light, and then she was gone.

Silence was left in her place. We all stared at the wall as the light began to shrink as swiftly as it had expanded. The mirror, or window, shrank away, and as the last of the light dimmed, the stone returned to its shiny black colour. There was no trace of Giselle, except for the gun she'd dropped as she'd vanished into nowhere.

"Ember?" Cori lifted her head, her voice groggy. "What happened? Where are we?"

Where to even start? "What do you remember?"

"The Stronghold." Her expression clouded. "The prison. But you… I can't be…"

"I got you out." I trod over to the Moonbeam but didn't quite dare touch it after Giselle's disappearance. "Malkin put you to sleep, and I had to use this to wake you up, but it…"

What had it done? Transported Giselle somewhere else? I had my doubts she was on the other side of the house, at any rate, but even Malkin hadn't mentioned the Moonbeam being able to act as a portal.

"That's…" Cori's eyes widened. "The Moonbeam."

"You know about it?"

"Malkin." She rocked back on her heels. "I remember him bragging about it when I was in jail. He said it could make shifters do whatever he wanted. And he said it was a direct link to the dragon shifters."

"What, the dragon shifters are on the other side of… that?"

Everyone stared at the wall, but the light did not return. The stone had returned to its former innocuous state, the faint sheen on its black surface the only sign of its magical nature.

"I don't know," said Cori. "The portal can only be used by a dragon shifter, and you have to focus on the location you want. I guess it opened for me because I was thinking about keeping you safe from… from that hunter. She was a hunter, right? She was holding a gun."

"Ex-hunter." Like Astor. Oh, hell. "She wanted to destroy the Moonbeam. Damn, she's going to be pissed off." If she ever found her way back.

Cori's brow wrinkled. "You'll have to fill me in. I've no idea where we are, or how I got out of the Stronghold, or… shit, I don't even know what day it is."

"Believe me, I have a few questions myself."

There came a loud rapping on the door. "Open up!" shouted a familiar voice.

Shit. Shit. "It's the mages."

Specifically, Lady Clare. How in hell had she found us?

"Then I'm dead." Astor spoke in a matter-of-fact tone, but his body was tensed, as though ready to run.

"No fucking way." I reached for the Moonbeam again, wincing at another loud rapping noise from the front door. We had seconds at most before they came in and killed Astor on the spot.

Unless I sent him elsewhere.

I gripped the Moonbeam in both my hands, concentrating on my need to save Astor. The stone's light grew bright, and a series of symbols danced before my eyes, almost like words flickering across the Moonbeam's surface too fast for me to read. The stone vibrated in my hands as I screwed up my eyes against the burning glare.

This time, the light hit the floor beneath Astor's feet rather than the wall. He swore, eyes widening as he fell through the burning glow..

An instant later, the door gave way with a crash and robed mages flooded into the room.

Shouts echoed off the walls. The Moonbeam flew from my hands, the light fading as I found myself yanked off the ground as if by an invisible force. Telekinesis? Whatever it was, my body was locked tight, arms pinned to my sides, the blood rushing to my head as I dangled six feet above where the Moonbeam lay on the bare floorboards. Around me, my friends hovered, similarly restrained.

"You're all under arrest," said Lady Clare. "If you resist, you'll be executed on the spot, so I'd advise you to cooperate."

The last flicker of light vanished. Astor was gone.

ABOUT THE AUTHOR

Emma is the New York Times and USA Today Bestselling author of the Changeling Chronicles urban fantasy series.

Emma spent her childhood creating imaginary worlds to compensate for a disappointingly average reality, so it was probably inevitable that she ended up writing fantasy novels. When she's not immersed in her own fictional universes, Emma can be found with her head in a book or wandering around the world in search of adventure.

Find out more about Emma's books at
www.emmaladams.com.